# FAIR CATCH

FAIR CATCH
A BEAUMONT SERIES NEXT GENERATION SPIN-OFF
HEIDI MCLAUGHLIN
© 2023

COVER DESIGN: OkayCreations.
EDITING: Edits by Amy
PROOFING: YR Editor
PHOTOGRAPHY: RplusMphoto
MODELS: Cody Smith / Jessica Pisarczyk

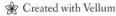 Created with Vellum

# THE PORTLAND PIONEERS:
# A BEAUMONT SERIES NEXT GENERATION
# SPIN-OFF

Fourth Down

Fair Catch

False Start

## THE BEAUMONT SERIES

# ONE

## KELSEY

When I packed up my life in New York and made the cross-country trek to Portland for the job of a lifetime, excitement and anticipation filled me. How different could one big city be from another? But then I arrived, and the gray skies opened, and the rain seemed endless.

"Good morning, Ms. Sloane." Barrett, the doorman for my building, nods to me while I stand under the awning and wait for a break in the foot traffic before opening my umbrella and stepping out.

Like when I lived in New York, I don't have a car. Portland's a city with a massive public transportation system. Why waste money on buying a car, paying for parking, and getting auto insurance? I'd much rather travel to different countries than spend money on something I'd rarely use.

"Morning, Barrett." I drop the "good" because nothing seems good at the moment. I get that it's fall, and I'm used to the chill in the air, but I'm also used to warm fall days and cool nights. This crap Portland is dumping on me makes me second-guess living here.

"It's for your dream job," I mutter to myself.

"What's that, Ms. Sloane?"

Shaking my head, I glance at Barrett. "Sorry, I'm trying to psyche myself up for the walk to work."

"Would you like me to hail you a cab?"

"No. But thank you. I need to get used to the rain."

Barrett laughs. "After a while, you won't even notice it."

*Whatever you say.*

When I see an opening between the hordes of people walking, I click the button on my umbrella and step out from beneath the awning. I shiver and pull my black trench coat tighter, wishing I could've worn my full-length peacoat since it's lined with wool and has always kept me warm. That coat will always be my favorite ever purchase, but a wet peacoat takes ages to dry.

Today, I'm thankful for the crowds gathered on the street corners. The ones that stand on the curb are brave. They're willing to get wet for the rest of us. Each time I see a car careening toward the curb for a coveted parking spot, I wait for the driver to hit the puddle, splashing the people waiting to cross. And the lengthy line of obscenities that are sure to come.

By the time I make it into my office, I'm bone cold. In my cubicle, I flip on the space heater I keep under my desk and hang my coat before heading into the breakroom. Thankfully, there's a pot of coffee brewed and ready for pouring. After I put my lunch in the refrigerator, I pour myself a cup and head back to my desk.

I'm early, in the sense that most of my coworkers roll in before noon. Many of them spend most of their nights staying up all hours reading manuscripts. Not me. I've never been much of a night owl, and literally can't read past nine p.m., which is pretty unreasonable since my job is to read manuscripts and decide if they are worthy of publishing.

I love my job as an acquisitions editor for an up-and-coming publishing house in Portland. Leaving my job in New York to join Willamette Publishing was the best decision for my career. It was their business model (and the fact they had landed the biggest authors on the planet) that had my bags packed before the ink dried on my contract.

The only thing I regret—the rain.

But like Barrett says, I'll get used to it.

My laptop boots up, and my email automatically opens. Each new message filters in. Twenty-five submissions overnight, and now sent to the printer. My boss complains about the amount of paper I use, but I'd much rather hold the sample in my hand and make notes than read it on my screen. My mentor is to blame. She taught me this way, and it's how I prefer to work.

The first one on my pile is from an agent I've worked with many times. Her clients haven't disappointed yet with their submissions. Except, this one throws me off kilter a bit. It's a sports romance, which is always a hot commodity. However, I don't know jack shit about football.

The submission is good. Great even. It has everything an editor looks for from story flow, pacing, conflict, and flirty banter, which I'm a sucker for. Give me the fun-loving jabs and I'm taking this to my boss. My only hang-up—the sports talk. Granted, I know what a tackle is, but the lingo leaves me wondering if the author is right or just blowing smoke.

This one goes into my "maybe" pile, and I work through the rest, asking for full reads on three of them, passing on a handful, and the rest I email the agent asking for some minor revisions. There were a couple I really enjoyed, but both had *something* missing. Those will usually come back to my email within days because the author is eager to land the deal.

I email the agent on the football one, explaining I need a couple of days to decide but ask for a full manuscript. I'm curious and the pitch was at the top of my list, but I need to make sure I know what I'm getting into before I take it to the higher-ups.

Back in the breakroom, I head to the refrigerator and grab my yogurt while I wait for the next pot of coffee to brew. Each of us has suggested we get one of those one cup brewers, but again, the cost and waste is a problem. The owner, Jonathan Tally, is very conscious about the amount of waste we create, which I get. He recycles everything, including the coffee grounds.

Basha Norris stands at the counter and drums her finger on the granite countertop. She's been at WP for a year, and while I mostly take contemporary romance, she's the historical queen in our small publishing house.

"What do they say about a watched pot?" she asks with a sigh.

"It doesn't boil," I reply. "Or brew."

"I should bring my own machine in. If I leave it at my desk and take my trash with me, Jonathan won't say anything, right?"

I shrug and lean against the counter with my empty mug in my hand. "He might. We could always ask."

"You know who'd have a problem with it?"

"Kit," I say with a sigh. She's the boss. Everyone loves her except she complains a lot about noise. The open office concept isn't for everyone, and on this floor, she's everyone. Someone sent Jonathan an anonymous note asking him to move Kit to an office, so the editors and staff could work in peace without Kit sending a mass email reminding everyone to keep their nails cut short because she hates the clickity clack they make on the keyboard.

"Right. The noise would bother her."

Finally, there's enough coffee in the pot for one cup and Basha pours herself one. "Sorry," she says with an apologetic look.

"I don't mind. Hey, let me ask you something. I received a pitch today and I like it, but it's in the sports romance category and I don't know jack about football. Should I have Jonathan read it?"

"Is it sporty or one of those 'he's an athlete, but they never actually detail anything about the sport' sort of thing? Because those annoy the crap out of me. I read one the other day about cricket and the bloke didn't play a single game or if he did, it was in the female POV, so she just gushed about his tight ass in his pantaloons."

"Is that what she called his pants?" I open my yogurt and start eating.

Basha nods and takes a sip of her coffee. She takes it black, no cream or sugar. Nothing fancy. She calls it her high-octane formula. "Yep. I don't know how many times I had to delete it from her MS only to find out the lead is British. It's one of those things where the author should mention it before I get click happy."

"Huh. Anyway, I think by the submission this is going to be detailed, which is great, but what if some of the terminology or game play is wrong?"

"Why don't you go to a game? We have a team here."

"I'm not sure that would help me understand the game. Like what does a tackle mean? Or a sack? Those were two words she used."

"Seasoned or new author?"

"New. Otherwise, I might let it go. I like the concept though, a lot."

"Oh!" Basha's dark eyes widen. "What if you interview the team or something?"

"Like an on-the-field reporter?"

"Sort of, I guess. I'm thinking more like the coach or someone giving you a crash course in all things football."

*Hmm.* "I like that idea a lot, actually. I wonder how I'd set that up?"

"Check with Valentine. I bet she can figure it out for you."

"I'll go see her after I fill this mug up." I rinse the yogurt cup and put it in the correct recycle bucket. "Thanks, Basha."

"Of course. Let me know how it goes." Basha exits the breakroom, leaving me there with my thoughts. I like the idea of being on the field or whatever. Firsthand knowledge is better than anything Google is going to give me.

After I fill my mug, I head to the other end of the floor, where our superhuman publicist, Valentine Geis, sits. She's typing frantically on her keyboard and bobbing to whatever she's listening to through her headphones. I stand in front of her cubicle to avoid scaring the crap out of her by tapping on her shoulder.

"Hey, what's up?" she asks after removing her headphones.

"Any chance you can set me up with an in-depth tour with the football team?" I fill her in on why.

"Which one?"

"We have more than one?"

Valentine laughs and nods. "Professional, college, and high school. Take your pick."

"Oh," I say, letting the "oh" linger a bit longer than I should. "Definitely professional. If not, any of the colleges would be fine."

"Let me see what I can do. I'll let you know. Is there a timeline?"

"The sooner the better. I'd like to get back to this agent and author soon. The story has a ton of potential, but for my peace of mind, I want my ducks in a row before I take it to Kit and Jonathan."

"You got it. I'll email you."

"Thanks, Valentine."

I head back to my desk and pull out one of my many red pens to start an edit on a project, only to have my email flash a few minutes later.

From: Valentine Geis <vgeis@WillamettePublishing.com>
To: Kelsey Sloane <ksloane@WillamettePublishing.com>
Subject: Today, 4:30

Kelsey,
Bud Walter, the coach of the Portland Pioneers, says you're welcome to attend practice today, if you're free. He'll have a player available for you to speak with after, as well.
Let me know and I'll confirm.
Valentine

Relief washes over me. I send my reply to Valentine and then minutes later she has all the information I need and tells me I'm going to meet with Myles, Coach Walter's assistant. She also writes that Myles is a flirt and doesn't hold back with his oversharing.

THE REST of the day drags on. I'm nervous and excited. Learning and experiencing something new is always high on my list of things to do, but this might be the most over-the-top thing I have ever done. Most would take an author's word for it or have a fact checker read over the story. I'm not most. I want firsthand knowledge of what I'm reading about. It gives the story a different feel.

Outside, I hail a cab and tell the driver where I'm going. The stadium is only a few blocks away, which I could've easily walked. But the parking lot stretches on forever. And ever. I swear it takes us longer to drive to the entrance of the stadium than it took to get to the gate.

There's a man waiting at the door for me and smiles as I approach. "Hello, are you Ms. Sloane?"

"Yes, please call me Kelsey." We shake hands.

"I'm Myles. I'm Coach Walter's assistant."

"Oh, you're one of the coaches?" I open the Notes app on my phone and start typing.

"No, I'm on the office side of things," he tells me as he leads me through the empty concourse. "I take care of everything, aside from anything that has to do with coaching. There's a whole other staff for that."

"Got it. Is this place always so empty?"

"Until the night before a game and game day. Then it's a madhouse. All our offices are on the top floor, with a view of the field. There's more life up there," he laughs as he presses the button on the elevator panel. "So, you're writing a story?"

"No, not me, but it's a potential story. I'm an acquisitions editor at Willamette Publishing. A submission came across my desk this morning about football, and I don't have a clue about the game, so I thought I'd poke around a bit."

"Gotcha. Well, let's start with the tour upstairs and then I'll take you over to the practice field."

"There's more than one field?"

Myles nods. "The grounds have a stadium, a practice field, as well as a field house with an indoor field. During the preseason, fans can come watch practices and scrimmages. During the off season, we allow people and other organizations to rent the space. It's great for conferences, and we have the parking to host large events."

"What else happens at the stadium?"

"A lot of concerts during the summer months. Conventions. You name it."

I type out the information on the stadium, even though I might not need it. It's still nice to have and might be something we can use in the future.

Despite the crappy weather, the team is outside practicing. Myles points out the offensive and defensive players, the quarterback, and the coaching staff. My fingers type rapidly, trying to keep up with everything he says. I'm hyper-focused on the quarterback and the lowdown Myles is giving me about him. I press record on my phone and film the action, only to drop my device at the sound of bodies crashing into each other.

"Let me grab that for you." Myles hands me my phone. Thankfully, the screen didn't scratch or crack.

"Was that a tackle?"

"Yes, but there's more than meets the eye when it comes to a tackle."

"What do you mean?"

"Well, for instance, the offensive linemen are trying to block the defensive linemen from getting to the quarterback, while the defensive backs are ready to tackle the offensive player down the field."

"Oh my, this is complicated."

"Come on, let's go out onto the field. If I can be honest with you, it's my favorite place to be."

"Why's that?"

"As odd as it may sound, I love feeling the thunder under my feet. Just wait."

The whistle blows again, and the same thing happens with the quarterback yelling, and then I get it. The players running together feel like thunder, and the crunch of them hitting each other reverberates and causes me to shiver.

"Oh, I get it now."

"Right? Plus, they're nice to look at."

"Who?"

"The men," he says with a shrug. Valentine was right. I don't know if I would ever admit my attraction to someone I just met, but he doesn't seem to care. Myles leans to the side and I do the same.

"Oh, I see," I say, agreeing with him. "Well, damn."

"Yeah, I enjoy my job." Myles chuckles.

Another much longer whistle sound blows and the guys take their helmets off. Some walk off the field, gather in a circle, walk toward the sideline, while one runs to their coach. They talk for a moment and then he makes his way toward us. Our eyes lock instantly. He smiles a bashful, crooked smile, and my knees go weak. I swallow hard as he approaches.

"Kelsey, this is Alex Moore. He's our center."

I don't have a clue what that means. I'm about to ask

when his meaty hand engulfs mine. "Hello, Ms. Sloane. I'm Alex and I'm going to give you the ins and outs of football. But first, I need to shower. Myles will keep you company and bring you to the locker room in thirty minutes." Alex winks and then heads toward the crowd moving toward the building. He doesn't give me a chance to respond, for which I'm thankful. I'm not sure I could muster any words over the lump I feel in my throat.

"Come on, I'll introduce you to Bud." Myles laughs and I know instantly he saw my reaction to the player. I can't help it. I am human after all.

## TWO

## ALEX

Coach Walter and his handy assistant, Myles, come into the weight room. None of us stop what we're doing, nor does anyone turn down the music. We keep lifting, jumping rope, and doing whatever the hell Jessie McAvoy, our right tackle, is doing.

Coach stands in the middle of the room, with his hands on his hips. He rarely says anything to us about our regimen, leaving that up to the professional trainers on staff, but sometimes he comes in and teases us about being weak or again, questioning Jessie and his obscure way of training. Today though, there's something on Coach's mind.

Myles stands next to him, decked out in Pioneer gear, and looking like he's up to no good. Everyone loves Myles. He's a hoot to hang out with and often asks one of us to accompany him to the bar to meet other men. There isn't a guy on the team who doesn't jump at the opportunity to be his wingman. We know he's using us to get attention, but we don't care. Honestly, sometimes it's fun to go out and just hang.

That's been my life lately. "Hanging" or whatever that's

supposed to mean. It has been since Maggie left for England and we broke up because of my unwillingness to leave my career for hers. The ask was too much, in my opinion. It's not like I'm some businessman grinding away with the nine-to-five. But she didn't see it that way.

Getting over her has been hard. Made more difficult by the text messages we continue to send back and forth, and the FaceTime chats we have late at night, or in her case, early in the morning. Maggie initiates them. When she told me she needed space—I gave it to her. Yet, she can't seem to let go. I don't know why I engage, and I should probably stop.

After what feels like ten minutes of him standing there, Coach finally yells for someone to shut the music off and gather around. Only, for those with headphones on, they're still pumping iron and all we hear is the clank of metal hitting metal and grunting.

I'll be honest, the grunting is a bit funny and uncomfortable to listen to.

"What's up, Coach?" Noah Westbury, our quarterback asks. I love Noah. He's one of my best friends. I chill a lot at his place, more so lately after my break-up. His wife, Peyton, works for the club and is a hard ass. She comes off as this tiny meek person, who barely makes a squeak, but she knows more about football than most of us and isn't afraid to tell us what kind of fuck ups we are on the field by pointing out all of your mistakes and showing you the error of your ways, in her equally soft voice. I've never feared anyone like I fear Peyton Westbury.

Myles clears his throat. "We have someone coming in to observe practice. She,"—Myles pauses and waits for the single men to get over their excitement—"needs the ins and outs of football. Her name is Kelsey, she's a book editor and doesn't know anything about the sport. One of you will meet with her after practice, talk to her, answer her questions, and most importantly, be on your best behavior."

The collective groan echoes throughout the weight room. Most of the guys slap Noah on his shoulder. He's normally our poster boy for anything charity related. Him or Julius Cunningham. Julius's popularity rose after he and our local meteorologist became a hot ticket item in Portland, but Noah and Peyton are the "it" couple. Their parents are uber famous and people think if they hang with them, they'll get to meet their dads.

"We're going to draw to see who Kelsey's tour guide is today. There are fifty-five pieces of paper in this box. One says winner. May the odds be in your favor."

"That's not the line, Myles," someone from the back of the room yells.

"The fact that you watched *Hunger Games* scares me," Myles shouts back.

One by one, we line up and die a little on the inside when the person in front of us declares they're safe from being the tour guide. When it's my turn, I take a deep breath. "Any words of wisdom?"

"Just draw the damn paper," Coach seethes. There's no doubt he's tired of our antics already.

I dip my hand into the box, twirl my fingers around a bit, and grab a piece of paper. My eyes close as my hands lifts the paper out of the box. I'm afraid to look. I should never be the person who has to explain football to anyone, but as luck would have it, *winner*, is scrawled across the small torn scrap of paper between my fingertips.

"Fuck."

Everyone behind me sighs heavily and then cheers loudly. I get a few pats on my back, some "atta boys," and a couple of my gracious teammates thank me for taking one for the team. As if I had a choice. I didn't volunteer. This forced labor is surely a violation of my contract. And if it's not, I'm going to make sure I add the clause during renegotiations.

"Kelsey will watch the last half of practice, and then she's all yours," Myles says.

"Great, does that mean I can take her into the locker room after practice and show her what football players *really* look like?" I waggle my eyebrows at him, and his face turns to stone.

"Don't be . . ." Myles sighs, pinches the bridge of his nose, and then shakes his head. I love goading him. He's a good cat for putting up with us lugs. "Alex—"

"Best behavior or it's the snake for three hours," Coach says. That gets me to change my attitude real quick.

"Kelsey, got it."

Coach and Myles leave with their heads bent together, likely talking about how I'm going to fuck this up because Maggie broke my heart. Truth is, she did. I thought we were in it for the long haul. I had asked the guys if I should ask Maggie to marry me and I had started looking at rings. It goes to show that despite being in love or saying you are, you're not always on the same page as your partner. Maggie taking the job in England stung. It still does. But I don't fault her for following her career path. It's exactly what I've done.

After more congratulatory slaps on my back, we head to lunch, and then will eventually make our way outside. Today's our slow day, or recovery day as I like to call it. We're going to walk through our plays after Peyton tells us we all suck, and then we'll hit a little bit. I could forgo the hitting part of practice. It's literally my least favorite thing in the world, which means I need to get faster at beating the defense down the field.

We all know the minute Kelsey is at the practice field. One of the guys whistles while another one mutters under his breath that he wished he could be her tour guide for the day. I almost hand over the reigns until I see her. She looks nervous, timid, and I think to myself it's probably a good thing she ended up with me because I'm as harmless as they come. Not that any of my teammates would do anything stupid, but sometimes their filter lacks when there's a lady around.

Coach calls an end to practice and yells for me to come see him. I take off my helmet and run to him, much like I did in high school or college. The entire moment feels like I'm trying to impress the cute girl on the sideline. Hell, maybe I am.

"Coach," I say as I approach.

"Myles found out that Kelsey is new in town. She's only been here a couple of months, moved from New York City."

"Well at least we know she's not a Jets or Giants fan." I laugh. Coach doesn't. *Tough crowd.*

"Anyway, answer her questions. Show her around the facility. Give her whatever she asks for."

"Anything?"

Coach rolls his eyes. "You know what I mean. You're representing the Pioneers. Make her fall in love with the sport. Hell, offer her tickets to the next game. She can sit in the booth, or we can give her a field pass. Just sell yourself and the sport."

"I can do that." I make my way toward the sideline where Myles stands with Kelsey. In two seconds flat, I smile like I've been caught with my hand in the cookie jar. She's gorgeous and far too pretty to hang out with the likes of me.

Myles nods toward me and says, "Kelsey, this is Alex Moore. He's our center."

This poor woman looks utterly confused. I don't give her time to think about whether she wants to shake my hand or not and reach for hers. It's tiny, dainty. I'm a giant compared to her. I could easily fit two of her onto my chest and probably leave room for another half person. She's the perfect little spoon.

I turn on the charm, or what I have left after Maggie took most of it, and say, "Hello, Ms. Sloane. I'm Alex and I'm going to give you the ins and outs of football. But first, I need to shower. Myles will keep you company and bring you to the locker room in thirty minutes." I have no idea why I repeat my name, but I have and it's out there. Before I leave her, I wink. The reaction I have confuses me. I'm not a flirt and have never been accused of being smooth, but apparently when you win a contest you didn't enter to show a beautiful woman around and tell her about your job, all the charm comes through.

Thirty minutes later, and after the guys gave me shit about the pixie waiting for me, I step out into the hallway to find Myles and Kelsey chatting it up. There isn't a doubt in my mind they'll be best friends by the end of the day. Myles is easy to get along with.

"All right, I'll leave you in the hands of Alex. It was nice meeting you, Kelsey. Email me if you need anything."

"Thank you, Myles."

Her voice is like a sweet song I could listen to on repeat, and I find myself with an unfamiliar feeling I can't explain. Nerves? Butterflies?

"Thank you for doing this," she says, looking directly into my eyes. I tower over her and have to bend down or step back to really see her. Through all my dating years, I've dated blondes and brunettes, but Kelsey, with her jet-black hair resting just below her shoulders in soft waves, has my full attention. I've never seen someone with deep, rich, brown eyes, but she has them and they gleam.

This isn't going to be a chore after all, but a blessing that I get to spend the rest of my afternoon with her.

"I'll be honest. We drew papers from a box, and I got the one that said winner."

She laughs and the cute squeak she makes goes right through every part of my body. "Lucky you."

"Definitely, lucky me."

The tour of the facility lasts an hour. She takes copious notes, asking me questions along the way. When we get out to the field, I detail everything. What the lines mean, the hash marks, etcetera, and then I get into the nuts and bolts of how the game's played. From the coin toss, to kick off. What happens at halftime, and then the end of the game, and how we have press conferences. I tell her about injuries, and how every day, something hurts, and we usually ignore it unless it could lead to something serious.

"And what do you do?"

"I'm the center." I take her out to the center of the field and have the equipment man bring out the dummies. "This is where I stand. My job is to hike the ball to Noah and then block the two guards—one on my right and the other on my left—from getting to him. He needs time to hand the ball off or throw it."

"Do you ever fail?"

"Of course, I do. I'm human. Everyone makes mistakes."

"And what happens if Noah gets tackled?"

"The quarterback gets sacked," I tell her. "It's still a tackle, because the defense tackled him to the ground, but it's called a sack."

"Oh, wow. This is confusing."

"I'm sure it is. Might I suggest you come to a game? I can set you up with someone who can explain the game to you as it happens."

Kelsey nods. "Yes, that might be a good idea. When do you play?"

I can't help the laugh that builds. "Mostly on Sundays. But sometimes we play on Mondays or Thursdays, and in January we might play on Saturdays."

"Why the switch in January?"

"Because college football is over in January and there's broadcast space to fill."

"Oh."

This poor woman looks thoroughly confused, and I feel sorry for her. "I don't want to be presumptuous here, but would you like to have dinner tonight? If you have a partner, bring them along. I feel like I can describe football and our plays better if we're sitting down, but I need to eat." I pat my thick belly. I'm not fat, but I'm not skinny either. But I like food and need to eat.

"That would be lovely."

"Great, I know a great little diner, not far from here. You can follow me."

"Actually, I don't have a car. I'll call for a cab."

"Or you can ride with me, if you'd like, and then I'll bring you home?"

Kelsey thinks about it for a moment, and then nods.

Outside, in the parking lot, Kelsey walks next to me. When we reach my truck, I help hoist her into it. For the first time since I had it tricked out, I hate and love it for the same reason. I hate that I had to touch her when she barely knows me but love that I had to touch her because I like the way she feels in my hands. Rushing around to the driver's side, I hop in and bring the souped-up engine to life. The roar is deafening at first and then calms down once in gear.

"This is a big truck."

"Yeah, sorry. I don't normally drive it, but I took a bunch of stuff to the dump for my neighbor this morning."

"That was kind of you."

"Thanks. She's an elderly lady and lives alone. During the season it's hard to do stuff for her, but in the off season, I mow her yard, clean her gutters, all the things her son should do for her."

"But he doesn't?"

"Nope," I say as I pull out into traffic. "He's a fifty something year old gamer and lives in the basement."

"Oh, that's shameful."

"Agreed. Okay, we're here."

"Well, this is very close."

"And convenient. I live about an hour away in the suburbs, so I usually stop here before I head back. Sometimes with traffic, it can be two hours before I'm home."

After shutting the truck off, I get out and go to the passenger side, and open the door. Kelsey looks at the ground. It's probably daunting for someone her size or for someone who isn't used to getting in and out of a lifted rig.

"Not to be forward, but it might be easier if I lift you out."

Kelsey nods and reaches for me. Except, it's not a hands on the shoulders sort of thing. It's a full arm wrap, almost as if she fears I'm going to drop her. I wouldn't. Ever. Holding her, having her pressed to my chest like this, sends a jolt of electricity through me. I can't help but look at her and wonder if she felt what I did. We look into each other's eyes and her fingertips play with the hairs on the nape of my neck.

Swallowing hard, I say, "I should probably put you down," in a low rumbly voice.

"Okay," she whispers. I don't do it. I don't put her down and, instead, continue to hold her like she's part of me now. The voice in my head tells me to kiss her, that she wants to be kissed by me. All I would have to do is pucker my lips and they'd press against hers.

"Alex! Oh my God, that's Alex Moore."

The moment is gone as a group of teenagers flock to us. I set Kelsey down and apologize for what's about to happen. No one should have to experience this.

# THREE

## KELSEY

> What do they call it when the sun shines and it's raining?

The text message from Alex makes me smile. I know it shouldn't, but I can't help it. At the end of our dinner meeting—not date—he asked for my phone number, and I gave it to him with zero hesitation. A first for me. Normally, I'm standoffish about people—and men in general. Being burnt by a few bad apples has left a sour taste in my mouth, especially when it comes to dating. Not that Alex and I are dating or anything, but damn it if my heart doesn't jump at the thought.

My eyes drift from my phone screen to my window where the sun is trying to peek through the curtains. I need to know the answer to Alex's question, but I also want to know if there's a reason why he's texting me. I kick my down comforter away like a child, rush to the window and throw my curtains open as if it's Christmas morning. It takes a second for my eyes to adjust but once they do, I marvel at the phenomenon.

> Wow!

I text back.

ALEX MOORE
> Crazy, right? It happens a lot here. It's called a sun shower.

> Consider me incredibly impressed. Thank you for letting me know.

ALEX MOORE
> You're welcome! What are you doing today?

> Um . . . working?

ALEX MOORE
> Well, if you need anything, please let me know.

> I will, thank you!

Why is my heart beating abnormally fast over a few text messages? I sigh and head into the bathroom to shower. After my encounter with Alex, and even Myles, I'm confident I can make an offer on the football romance story. Of course, after I discuss it at our team meeting. Kit has to approve everything, and while we're pitching our stories to her, the rest of us discuss what sort of marketing we can do to help our client. Marketing is so important whether it's social media, book fairs, or in-store book signings. We, as publishers, need to do our part while the author does theirs.

Barrett opens the door for me as I approach, tipping his hat in greeting as he does so. "Good morning, Ms. Sloane."

"Good morning, Barrett. What a beautiful day."

He apprises me. "It's raining. Again." He points to the wet ground.

"But the sun's shining."

"Yes, that does make a difference. Are you walking today? Or would you like me to hail you a taxi?"

"Walking." I hold my umbrella up for him to see, and then press the button to open it. "Have a nice day, Barrett."

"You too, Ms. Sloane."

Once again, I'm walking among the others heading to work or to their meetings. Most of us wear earbuds. Some are talking, albeit a bit too animatedly for my liking. A couple of people are bobbing their heads and I wonder what they're listening to. Right now, my current listen is 80's love songs. I don't know what it is, but they're my jam. And if I'm not careful, I'll be singing and bobbing my head right along with the rest of my walking cohorts.

After swiping my badge to get through security, I stand and wait for the elevator. Kit walks toward me and smiles. "Good morning, Kelsey."

"Good morning." As far as bosses go, she's pretty awesome. We met at a conference in Florida and hit it off. She sold me on this baby publisher and encouraged me to apply for a job. I didn't at first because the idea of moving coasts wasn't appealing, but here I am.

"Production meeting this morning. Are you ready?"

Internally, I groan. For the most part I don't mind the meetings, until it's my turn. I don't mind selling new books to the team but loathe when we talk about sales numbers. Sometimes, we love a book, but something inevitably gets in the way of making it a bestseller. It's hard to pinpoint why readers will pick up a book and why they won't. It's not like we can stand on a street corner asking people. Although now that I think of it, maybe we could.

"Yes, I have a pitch to present."

"Great," Kit says enthusiastically. "I'm excited to hear it."

*No pressure.*

We get into the elevator and Kit presses the button. When we reach our floor, we greet Robin, our receptionist. At my cubicle, I leave my stuff and head into the breakroom for my much-needed coffee and to put my lunch into the refrigerator.

"Hey," Valentine says when I step into the room. "How did it go yesterday?"

"Great. Fantastic, really. Myles was great and so was Alex." My cheeks heat up at the mention of his name.

"What!? Girl, I need some details."

"About what?" I shrug and pretend I have no idea what she's talking about.

"Oh, nah. Stop hiding. Alex? What's his last name?" Val pulls her phone out and looks at me expectedly.

"Moore," I tell her. "He's the one who gives the ball to the quarterback."

"Noah Westbury is our quarterback. I have a crush on his dad."

"Who's his dad?" I ask.

"Liam Westbury, lead singer of 4225 West."

*Yep, total crush.* "Who doesn't?" I mutter.

"Alex Moore," Valentine says his name in a hushed tone. "Says here he's recently single."

"Oh?" My interest piques when I shouldn't care. We didn't talk about anything other than football during dinner. Not about his life or mine, but about the game and how it's played. After we finished, he drove me home and asked for my number. Sure, I felt the connection between us, but it's probably one-sided.

*But was it?*

With my mug in my hand, I pour my coffee, leaving room for creamer. "How did you set the meeting up so soon?"

"Myles is my roommate," Valentine tells me. "He was so thrilled to do it because it would annoy the guys."

"Alex seemed happy to show me around."

"Of course, he was. The guys are genuinely really great, but they whine like children when they have to do something. Still, they do it and never complain."

"Well, it was eye-opening, so thank you. And like I said, Myles was great."

"He liked you too."

Valentine and I make our way to our respective cubicles, and I do what I probably shouldn't and Google Alex. I bypass his Wiki and player profile on the Pioneers page and click on the image tab. Photo after photo fill my screen, along with categories: Wallpaper, NFL Combine, Noah Westbury, high school, cool, charity, and Maggie Gardner. Stupidly, I click on Maggie and a flood of images pop up of her and Alex. Some intimate. Him nuzzling her neck. Them in an embrace. Them kissing.

My heart drops despite Valentine's voice echoing, "Says here he's recently single."

I type out, Alex Moore and Maggie Gardner break up, and hit enter.

One link. I click and Twitter opens.

- *PPFan4life: OMG! My heart. Alex and Maggie broke up.*
- *SuperBowler123: No, there's no way. They're aisle bound*

- *SianPioneers: They haven't been seen together in months.*
- *PPFan4life: And Maggie's living in London.*
- *JPLovesFootball: Hello, British boys!*
- *SianPioneers: Ugh, no! Alex is perfect.*
- *JPLovesFootball: No way, give me Chase!!*
- *NoahsNo1Fan: Noah!!*
- *4225Wester: Harrison!!!!!*
- *PPFan4life: This thread is getting off track. Keep to Alex and Maggie or I'll delete.*
- *NoahsNo1Fan: Such a bitch. It's a sub convo.*
- *PPFan4life: Bite me.*
- *SianPioneers: Tickets for the game, I'm making a sign I love you, Alex.*
- *SuperBowler123: He'll never see it. Besides, he loves Maggie.*
- *PPFan4life: OMG do you remember when he told the reporter he wanted to marry her?? Swoon!!!!*
- *JPLovesFootball: He's too big for me. I like them skinny.*
- *SianPioneers: You're watching the wrong sport.*
- *Jenny_notfromtheblock: I like my men thick.*
- *SianPioneers: Alex is thick – if you know what I mean.*
- *Jenny_notfromtheblock: You don't know jack shit.*

I exit out of twitter and go back to looking at photos of Maggie. She's perfect in the way I strive to be but never will. My job doesn't require power suits, and no one is eagerly sending me gala invites. It takes me hours to get my hair to curl and that's if I add a ton of product. Not Maggie though, with her perfectly curled blonde hair, svelte figure, and picture ready image.

*Blah.*

The alarm on my phone goes off, reminding me it's time for our production meeting. I gather my files and laptop and head into the conference room. I'm kicking myself for feeling a little under prepared. When I should've been preparing, I was too busy Googling a man I just met and obsessing over his ex.

Thankfully, I'm last on the list to present, which gives me a few minutes to put some key points down. When it's my turn, I talk about the five offers I want to make, and in a surprise move Jonathan, not Kit, gives me the approval I need to move forward with three of them. One being the football story.

Valentine bumps my arm as we're leaving. "Looks like you'll have another excuse to see Alex." She winks and my insides do a twist. I want to see Alex again, even though it might be unprofessional.

"Yes, he offered to help so that'll be great."

"Maybe he'll read the first draft."

I laugh aloud. "Oh, can you imagine?"

"Actually, yes. I can. It'd be amazing marketing and I'm here for it."

"Oh," I pause. "Yes, I guess that would be good."

"I might have to run this one by Myles if the author takes your offer. Let me know."

Back at my desk, I send an email to the agent with our offer. It's a little on the low side, but this is a debut author and I'm doing this without having read the full manuscript. It's not how I always operate, but there are times when you have a good feeling about a story.

Once that's sent, I print off the new submissions I

received overnight and start going through them, breaking only to eat lunch and return emails. Of the three offers I made, one wants to negotiate a higher advance. I reply with a counteroffer, which I think is fair, but have a feeling the agent is going to pass. It won't be the first time this has happened. In this business, you win some, lose some.

Toward the end of my day, my phone vibrates, and Alex's name shows on the screen. It takes me a couple of rings before my brain and hand sync up. "Hello?" I say as I walk as fast as I can to one of our private rooms where all phone calls need to happen so I don't disturb the other editors.

"Hey, Kelsey. Am I catching you at a bad time?"

"Not really. Just reading over book submissions."

"Really? Do you get a lot?"

"Sometimes," I tell him. "Today, it's ten. Yesterday, twenty-five."

"With the football one?"

"Yes, that was yesterday. I made an offer on it," I tell him.

"That's awesome. Maybe you want to tell me about it at dinner tonight?"

*Yes, yes I do.*

I really liked being in his company yesterday and while my stomach may be twisting around, my heart jumps at the idea of spending time with him. If anything, he's going to be a good friend and someone who can help me make this book successful.

"What do you have in mind?"

"There's an amazing Italian place near my house. I could come pick you up after practice, and then I'll drive you back home."

"That sounds like a lot of trouble."

Alex chuckles. "Something tells me you'll be worth the trouble, Kelsey."

My stomach, heart, and every other vital organ hits the floor with a thud and has a dance party.

"I'm not sure what to say."

"Say you'll have dinner with me tonight."

"Yes, of course."

"Great, does six work?"

"Six is perfect," I tell him. "I'll wait for you at the door so you can pull up and not have to worry about parking."

"This is a date, Kelsey. I'll park and go into the lobby, and then I'll call you so you can buzz me up. Then, I'm going to knock on your door and hand you the flowers I will have purchased."

*A date.*

"Oh, um, okay. I'll wait for you in my apartment."

"See you at six, Kelsey." Alex hangs up before I can say anything. I stay in the private room and do a little dance before straightening my clothes and heading back to my desk. Except, I bypass my cubicle and head right to Valentine's and tell her all about the conversation, squealing as quietly as I can when I get to the part about the flowers.

## FOUR

## ALEX

"**G**ood evening," I say to the doorman. "I'm here to see Kelsey Sloane."

"Yes, sir, go ahead. There's a house phone near the elevators."

"Thank you." He holds the door for me, and I step into the lobby and look around. Every secure apartment building looks different from others. With Noah's, you have to check in at the receptionist's desk and get your picture taken before you're even allowed to go through the locked gate. Even if he calls down and tells the person sitting at the desk that he's expecting you and it's okay to send you up, they still follow the procedures they have in place.

*Gotta appreciate security.*

I pull my cell phone out of my pocket and call her.

"Hey," she says. "I'm 505. I'll buzz you in now."

Kelsey hangs up before I can ask her how everything works. The elevator opens and I step in. There are no buttons to press, only a card slot. "Interesting," I say to the empty car.

When I get to the fifth floor, it's a right down the hall.

I'm thankful she left her door shut because for some odd reason, I really want to knock and have her answer. Call me old-fashioned or whatever it might be. Although, I also like seeing someone waiting for me while leaning against the door frame. I guess that makes me a walking contradiction when it comes to what I like.

Standing in front of her door, I look at the 505 and smile before taking a deep breath, knocking, and holding the flowers I bought at the center of my chest. My lips move from a smile to no smile, and then back again. It's my hope that my smile seems endearing and not at all creepy. Believe me, I get the over-eager smile, and I often have one, especially during photoshoots or fan meet and greets. I know the line, "Alex you need to relax," all too well.

The door swings open, and she's there, her focus moving from me to the flowers and then back to me again. Her grin slowly spreads across her face, and I know I've done well. "Hi," she says breathlessly. I swallow hard and force myself to look at her instead of staring. Kelsey's wearing a black and blue dress, with a deep v-cut that accents the valley between her breasts. *Eyes up top, mister.* "Would you like to come in?"

"Of course." My hand extends, almost shoving the flowers into her chest. "Sorry, I'm nervous."

"Really?" Kelsey takes the bouquet and inhales their fragrant scent. "You weren't nervous the other day. Or were you?"

*Is she not?*

"I wasn't, and I think it's because yesterday was a job, so to speak." Her face falls, but she nods. "I'm not saying being with you felt like work because I had a great time teaching you about the game, but it was a work assignment. If that makes sense. Tonight, it's a date, and I'm trying to make a good impression."

Kelsey's eyes light up and she gives me a shy smile before turning away slightly. "You're making a very good first impression."

"Phew." I wipe away the imaginary sweat from my forehead. "I work hard to lose the dumb jock stigma."

"I don't even know what that is," she tells me. "I've never hung out with a jock."

"Never? Not even in school? None of your friends played sports?"

Kelsey shakes her head. "Not really. I knew a few, but we never spent time together outside of the classroom or school. I'm going to put these beautiful flowers in some water. Feel free to look around."

She disappears behind a corner, leaving me in her living room. I do look around because she encouraged me, but I'm very careful about what I touch because everything is white. Or maybe it's off white? Or cream? I haven't a clue but she's the exact opposite of me with my black couch and dark wood furniture. Along the main wall, she has a floor-to-ceiling entertainment center. Her flat screen television sits between bookcases filled with not only books, but other personal items, like awards, figurines, and statues that I assume are bookends.

"Do you like to read?" she asks from behind me. I startle at the sound of her voice and turn quickly to face her.

"Sometimes. It's hard during the season because I'm focused on the playbook and preparing for each team we face. During the off season, I'll read a book or two. What type do you edit?"

"Contemporary romance or women's fiction."

"Can't say I've ever read one of those." I chuckle.

"Maybe you can read the football one when I get it from the author."

*Or you can read it to me!*

"Yeah, sure. We want to make sure it's as accurate as possible."

"Exactly," she says as she comes and stands next to me. Kelsey picks up one of her awards. "One of the books I edited debuted on the New York Times bestseller list and the publisher I worked for gave this to me. It's one of my greatest achievements."

"How many times has that happened?"

"Just the once. The market . . . it's saturated and it's very hard for authors to get the attention they deserve without them or their publisher pumping tens of thousands into ads, and even those aren't guaranteed."

"Well, once is better than nothing."

"It really is. It's a massive feat for everyone involved."

"And this one?" I point to another award.

"My author reached a million sales. I had this made for her and made myself one as well to mark the accomplishment."

"Your publisher didn't?"

She shakes her head. "Willamette Publishing does. It's the reason I took the job with them. They treat their authors extraordinarily well. They mark occasions like birthdays and holidays, and send flowers on release days. Authors appreciate it and work harder. Editors appreciate it because it makes our authors happy. And when it comes to writing, happiness is important."

"Being happy is important no matter what," I say. "You have a beautiful place."

"Thank you." Kelsey looks around. "It's slowly coming together."

"Shall we go?"

She nods. "Let me grab my coat."

I follow her to the closet and help her into her coat before holding the front door open for her. Once she locks the door behind us, I guide her down the hall with my hand on her back and press the button to call the elevator. When we get outside, she waves to the door attendant and then pulls up short when we reach my car.

"Um . . . new car?"

"No, this is my regular car." I don't know how much a Model S Tesla can be thought of as a regular car considering the charging needed but it's this or hoisting her up into my truck again. Not that I wouldn't mind helping her get into my truck, but I think I'll save the somewhat sexual touching for date number three. I open the door for her and wait for her to slide into the passenger seat. If she's anything like me, she'll appreciate the buttery soft leather seats. They're one of my favorite things about my car.

"You don't strike me as a save the planet type of guy," she says when I get behind the wheel and press the brake pedal to start my car.

"I'm not," I say before I realize how my answer could be taken out of context. "What I mean to say is, I do my part by recycling, ensuring my home is energy efficient, and all that. I bought this car for my parents, but my dad didn't like all the techy stuff. Said it freaked him out and he didn't like my mom watching movies while he drove."

Kelsey laughs and covers her mouth. "If it were me, I'd end up reading."

"Believe me, as much as I don't like to do it, I let Rizzo drive for me because I'll watch highlights from a game or do a live session on Instagram or TikTok."

"Rizzo?"

I shrug and signal to turn. "My mom named her, and I didn't have the heart to change her name. Mom's a huge fan of *Grease*. Have you seen the movie?"

"I have, although it took me this year to realize what they're singing about. I guess, when I was younger, I was enamored with the characters and the movie, but I never paid attention to the lyrics of the songs. Now, when I hear them I blush, and wonder what in the hell my parents were thinking when they let me watch this movie for hours on end."

I can't help but laugh. "I heard this is a realization for fans later in life. I guess we'll have to watch it so you can make sure I fully grasp what I'm hearing."

"I can do that," Kelsey says shyly. I'll be honest, I like that she's already agreed to another date.

Rizzo turns onto another street and begins the uphill climb to my neighborhood. "Look behind you."

Kelsey turns in her seat and then lets out a whispering, "Wow."

"If you're up for it after dinner I'd love to show you the view from my house."

"Of course, unless it's late. I don't want to keep you from—"

"I'm all yours, all night," I interrupt her and hope she doesn't read too much into what I said. I'm not trying to get her to spend the night, but I also don't have a curfew and it's not like our night needs to end at nine or ten.

I pull into the parking lot and find the first available spot. After parking, I help Kelsey out of the car and keep my hand on the small of her back as we make our way into the restaurant. "Hi, I have a reservation for Alex Moore," I tell the host when it's our turn.

"This place is quaint," Kelsey leans into me and speaks.

"It's an old Victorian converted into a restaurant. If our table is upstairs, you'll see a dumbwaiter in action. It's pretty neat."

"How did you know I've never seen one before?"

"Wild guess," I tell her. The host tells us to follow him, and I rejoice a bit when he takes us to the staircase. I motion for Kelsey to follow behind him which is a major mistake because I'm two steps behind her and my eyes don't leave her backside and every swing of her hips gives me a little more to fantasize about.

When she reaches the top of the stairs, she looks over her shoulder at me. She smiles and extends her hand for me to take. I do so, without hesitation and link our fingers together. No more of my hand on her lower back, although I do like the feel of having it there.

The host holds Kelsey's seat for her, and I feel unnecessarily angry. It's an unfamiliar feeling because the times I've been here with Maggie, I never seemed to care. But with Kelsey—holding the chair out for her is something I want to do. I don't want to share her with anyone or have someone else on the receiving end of the look of gratitude she's currently giving the host.

I sit down with a huff and Kelsey glances my way, none the wiser of my internal battle. She opens her menu and as the waiter approaches, I tell him what wine we'd like, hoping I'm not being a total dick by ordering for her. As soon as he's gone, I set my menu down and clear my throat.

"I'm sorry, I should've asked if you even like wine. I apologize for assuming."

"You're fine, Alex. If I wanted something differently, I would've spoken up."

"Okay, good. That's good. I want you to always speak your mind when you're with me."

Kelsey smiles. "What's good here."

I spend the next five minutes or more, listing off my favorite dishes, which is really anything from the menu. When the waiter returns with our wine, we place our order. Kelsey picks up her glass and I do the same.

"I propose a toast," I say and then lose my train of thought because of the way she's looking at me, or maybe it's the way the small lights around us make her eyes look like they're sparkling. "To new friends and new adventures."

"I like new friends and new adventures," she says as she touches her glass to mine. When she takes a sip, her eyes never leave mine.

# FIVE

## KELSEY

*hy does this man affect me so?*

W This is easily the best Italian dinner I've ever had and that's saying something considering I moved here from New York City. Except, it's not the food. It's the company. It's Alex who makes the meal stand out over every other dinner I've had. He's funny, sweet, and caring. When he ordered wine for us, the thought never crossed my mind that I would want something else. It's odd to trust someone so fully, right after meeting them, but I do with him. Alex has an air about him. He's this big, burly type of man, who could crush me like a grape, but his demeanor screams gentle giant.

Toward the end of dinner, he reaches across the table and touches my cheek. His caress is soft, thoughtful. Gazing into his brown eyes, I see kindness and longing. On the tip of my tongue, sits the questions plaguing my mind from earlier—Maggie. Why did they break up? Is he over her? By all accounts, he was in love. Is he still? I know I'm getting way ahead of myself in thinking there might be something between us, but I feel it. Deep in my bones, I feel a connection. It's unlike anything I've ever felt before.

When the check comes, Alex insists on paying, even though I offered to pay for half. He's by my side, guiding me down the stairs. They're carpeted and not great for heels. Yet, I'd feel like a shrimp standing next to him if I didn't give myself a little bit of height. Even now, he towers over me. The difference between us, which is well over a foot, should scare me, but I feel safe when he's around. No one is going to mess with him, or me for that matter.

He holds my hand as we walk through the parking lot and opens the car door for me. He's a gentleman, through and through. Polite, courteous, and sweet. When he slides behind the steering wheel, his artificially intelligent car adjusts to him, and the computer greets him. I catch him smiling. This guy is a softy.

"I'm going to let Rizzo drive us to the nearest coffee shop."

"Okay?" I look at him questioningly. He tells Rizzo where he wants to go and then puts his car in drive. I should probably panic at the sight of seeing the steering wheel turn without his guidance, but I don't. He's still behind the wheel and I suppose somewhat in control. Yet, he's looking at me.

"I'm not drunk or anything," he tells me and now I understand. "But I do question whether we left too early."

"I get it."

"So, we're going to go get some coffee."

"Sounds like the perfect ending to a perfect night."

My words take him by surprise. "This was a perfect night for you?"

"Yes."

"Was it the food?"

I shake my head slightly and wet my lips, in hopes he'll kiss me. "The company."

A small smile spreads across his face. Alex tilts his head and leans forward. Kissing while your AI drives you someplace feels odd, and out of the norm, but I go with it. Unfortunately, Rizzo picks that moment to announce our arrival and now Alex has to focus on parking or whatever needs to be done.

The moment is over. Lost in the abyss of stupid technology and late-night coffee shops. Still, he holds my hand as we make our way into the shop. It's self-seating and he leads us to a booth by the window. The street is quiet, and the view is spectacular.

"I can't believe how beautiful the city looks from up here."

"It's gorgeous until you get downtown," he says.

"Can I be honest about something?"

"Always." Alex reaches for my hand. His thumb moves back and forth over the top of my hand. My fingertips are cold—well they were, until he warmed them with his soft grip.

"I'm shocked at the way downtown is. I expected better," I tell him. "I know NYC isn't the best, but Portland just seems worse. I tried to explore the downtown area and felt unsafe."

"It's all politics, and the mayor is unwilling or unable to do anything about crime, drugs, and homelessness. It's sad because I, too, expect more. I know the owner of the Pioneers donates a ton of money to revitalization efforts, but every year, the funds are commingled or there's some emergency that has to be dealt with first. It's infuriating."

"I want to love it here, but I don't know."

"Are you from New York?"

Nodding, I add, "Upstate. A very small town with absolutely nothing around it."

"Did you always want to work in publishing?"

"I did. Growing up in a small town, you either played sports or you were the 'nerd' of the school. I was the nerd. My hand-eye coordination isn't great, so I studied a lot, and when I wasn't studying, I read." I shrug. "The progression into publishing seemed like the right path for me."

"Where did you go to college?"

"Rochester Institute of Technology. I have a BS in English, with a minor in creative writing and immersions in digital literature, and comparative English."

"So, you enjoy writing?" he laughs.

"Not at all. I can't string two coherent sentences together, but I can help an author make their sentences stronger."

The waitress comes over with two mugs and a carafe of coffee. "Can I get you guys anything?"

"May we see your dessert menu?" Alex asks her. She nods and turns away. "This is coffee," he continues. "It's okay. Not great. It might put hairs on your chest, but the pie here is decent. I come here a lot because no one ever seems to find me here."

"And they find you at Starbucks?"

"Without a doubt."

"I'm sorry, that must get annoying."

Alex shrugs. "It's not as bad as some of the guys. Like Noah, our quarterback. I don't remember if I told you or not, but his dad is famous. He's the lead singer for 4225 West, and to make matters worse, Noah's married to Peyton, who's dad is the drummer of the band. Plus, her brother has a band. They can't go anywhere without the paparazzi following them or fans hounding them. I feel sorry for them, sometimes."

"Only sometimes?"

Alex laughs and shrugs. He pours us each a cup of coffee and then pulls the ceramic box of sugars over, along with the cream.

"Okay, you know about me. Tell me about you. Where are you from and where did you go to school?"

He takes a sip of the coffee and shakes his head with a grimace. "That's strong," he says before taking another sip. "Okay, about me. I'm from Detroit. I was a rough and tumble kid, always in trouble. When I was twelve, my parents moved us to the 'burbs because they thought I was going to join a gang.

"A gang? That seems extreme."

Alex nods. "Sometimes my mom can be over the top, ya know. Like takes everything to the extreme. Once we moved, I started playing football then, thanks to my neighbor, and found out I was actually pretty good at it. In high school, I shot up in height, and started lifting weights. Ended up with a full scholarship to Iowa State, and then after four years there the Pioneers drafted me."

"Do you like playing?"

"I love it." Alex takes the ceramic box of sugars between his hands and turns it around absentmindedly. "The team is my family. Some of us are tighter than others, but at the end of the day, I have fifty-one brothers who have my back."

"Do you have any other siblings?" I ask, needing to know more about him as a person and not a player.

He nods. "I have a sister. She lives near my parents. She's married and has two kids, one of each. I love my niece and nephew a lot and enjoy spoiling the crap out of them because it irks my sister. What about you?" Alex leans closer to me, which isn't hard since the table is so small.

"Two brothers, Davy and Dalton. No nieces or nephews and no prospects of having any either. They're both single, much to my mother's dismay. I'm the baby of the family. Davy lives in Florida. Dalton travels for work a lot so he stays with our parents when he's in the area for any extended amount of time."

"Siblings are fun," he says as his finger caresses my hand. I like that he's flirtatious with me. "My sister is two years older than me and when I got to high school, I had all these hotties coming up to me. She put a kibosh on them right off. It wasn't until she graduated that I finally went on a date. All the girls in school were afraid of her."

I snort and cover my mouth. "Let me tell you, having older brothers isn't much different. My high school boyfriend was deathly afraid of Dalton. Still, Tanner was brave enough to ask me out. I think it helped that he was somewhat friends with Davy."

The waitress comes back with our menus. I look over the offerings and choose apple pie, while Alex goes for the chocolate mousse.

Alex clears his throat and then meets my gaze. "Is this Tanner back home, pining for you? Or anyone else I should know about?" he asks softly.

I shake my head slowly. "Nope. There's no one waiting and no one coming here."

Alex nods and leans forward. "I like you a lot, Kelsey. But I want to be honest here. I'm coming off a break-up. It wasn't something I wanted or even saw coming. I thought we were a solid couple and played with the idea of proposing, but she wanted other things. Things I can't or won't provide for her." Alex leans back and sighs. "I'm telling you this because if you're going to be with me, in any capacity, you'll hear about my ex, and I don't want you to be surprised by any of it."

*Do I tell him I already know?*

"Since we're being honest, I already Googled you and saw you and Maggie together. It seems you have a fanbase where the two of you are—or were—concerned. I have to ask though, are you over her?"

Alex leans forward again and takes my hand in his. "I didn't think I was, and then I met you yesterday. It's odd. I've spent so much of my time, thinking about Maggie, that I think I forgot how to live without her. And then, I meet you, and it's like the sun's shining again, despite it being a cold and dreary fall.

"I'm not going through the motions as if I'm in a rut but embracing my routine. This morning, when I woke, I thought about you and couldn't wait to call to ask you to dinner. All morning, I paced and wondered when it would be appropriate to call. I didn't want to wake you up, ya know. Asking you out to dinner has been one of the easiest things I've done in a long time. Also, one of the most nerve-racking."

"How come?" I ask quietly, unable to find my voice after listening to him. His words are true, genuine, and whatever happened between him and Maggie, hurt him.

"I was afraid you had a boyfriend or say no."

My stomach flutters. The sensation isn't lost on me. It's been a long time since I've felt butterflies for someone. "Saying no never crossed my mind," I tell him. "I was so enamored with you that I looked you up this morning. I'll admit, knowing and reading about Maggie—it scares me."

Alex adjusts and takes my other hand in his. "I'm not that kind of guy, Kelsey."

The waitress brings our desserts and another carafe of coffee. Alex offers me a bite of his. The cool chocolate rests nicely on my tongue. I give him a bite of my warm apple pie with a spoonful of ice cream. He moans as he takes my spoon into his mouth.

"So good."

"You like your sweets?"

He nods. "It's an indulgence. During the season, I'm normally strict with my diet, but tonight is a special occasion."

I take a bite and match his earlier expression. "I don't think I've had something so delicious. I think they soaked the apples in cinnamon. Remind me not to tell my mom."

Alex laughs. "As long as you don't tell mine that I moaned when I tasted your pie."

The air around us shifts at the sexual innuendo. My ankles cross and my thighs tighten with the thought of Alex and me together. I hadn't imagined anything like that between us, but now, the thoughts filter through like a mirage with our bodies tangling. My leg over his hip. Him thrusting into me and his back arched.

As if he knows what I'm thinking, he caresses my cheek, bringing my attention back to the forefront. Before I can register his action, he's leaning over the table and pressing his lips to mine. They're soft, tentative, and welcoming. I begin to open for him, but he stops and sits back down.

"Well, now that the first kiss is out of the way, we'll be smooth sailing from here on out." Alex winks and takes a bite of his pie. His eyes roll back, and I find myself once again, imagining him, hovering over me.

# SIX

## ALEX

It's game day. I invited Kelsey, and even sent some Pioneer gear to her house, but she's not here. She also didn't say whether she would come or not, but I hope she will. Hell, I hope she'll miraculously appear in the stands. Of course, I probably should've secured some general tickets instead of putting her with the other wives and girlfriends. Initially, I thought she'd find something in common with them and become friends with a few. Thinking back, I should've had two tickets put aside for her so she could bring a coworker or something.

My head drops. I'm dense.

I could be reading the room wrong too. We have chemistry. There isn't a doubt in my mind there's something between us. It could be more on my end though. I've really enjoyed my time with her.

But then there's Maggie.

Kelsey knew about her, which isn't surprising. Everyone Googles everyone these days. It's the smart thing to do, especially if you're a woman who's just moved to a new city. It's something I'd want my sister to do if she ever dated again. Actually, background checks should be accessible to the public. That would definitely curb some of the crime out there.

The game starts and I make my way to the twenty-yard line. I'm slow moving and mentally kick my ass for not thoroughly thinking my actions through. The possibility I put Kelsey in a potentially uncomfortable situation never crossed my mind before now. She deserves better than that.

After a series of plays, I'm on the bench, pretending to listen to our offensive coordinator, and not hearing a single thing he tells us. I nod when everyone else nods, and then I go out and do my job.

When the horn sounds for halftime, I'm relieved. *Halfway done.* I jog my way toward the locker room, with some of my teammates patting me on my back for a job well done. I'm not sure what I did in the first half of the game that stood out to them, but I'll take it. I need the ego boost right now because I can't seem to get out of my own mind.

In the locker room, I head toward the bathroom. Taking a leak during the game is probably the most refreshing thing we can do. Except, it's near impossible until halftime. It's not like we can run off the field whenever nature calls. Nor can we assume the other team is going to march down the field, giving either the offensive or defensive line a long enough rest so we can run into the locker room to relieve ourselves.

When I was a rookie, I had the worst experience of my life. I had to piss like a racehorse. I asked every coach on the sideline what I should do. Most of them gave me some bullshit answer, like do a slow trickle or grab a handful of towels and go hide in the corner. Neither of those options seemed like the best choice, and at the time I figured they were hazing me because it was my first year.

Nope. It turns out, many NFL'ers do whatever they can to relieve themselves while still playing the game. Not me. My dumbass thought it would be a brilliant idea to use the bathroom for the people who have on-the-field passes. I rushed in, unaware that cleats and tile flooring don't mix, fell on my ass and skidded across the floor. I tried to use my hands to stop my momentum, but I had gloves on, and they were sweaty. Needless to say, the person standing at the urinals caught every second of my blunder and ended up hitting my leg with a steam of warm piss. Not to be deterred. I stood up, undid my pants, and did what any man in my situation would do. I nodded toward him and asked, "How's it hanging?"

Not my finest moment.

But one I've made sure to never ever repeat again.

Ever.

Because of this, I've limited my water intake during the game. It's not advisable, and the Pioneers trainer doesn't like it, but I have to do whatever it takes to keep my bathroom antics off social media.

Coach is drawing on the whiteboard like a frantic man when I come back into the meeting room. Most of the guys mumble in agreement with him when he asks a question. More often the questions are rhetorical, but the coaching staff pays attention to who is listening. It's nice when we're winning because Coach reminds us of what we need to do to continue—strong defense, smart passes—shit like that.

I go around the room and pat my offensive line on their shoulders to hype them up. We're doing a great job. Westbury hasn't been sacked once. And we've only had ten yards in penalties. That's a win in my book. Now, we just have to take our first half momentum into the last half of the game. We have to dig deep and hold the line.

We jog back onto the field, and I do everything I can not to look in the direction of where Kelsey should be sitting. I fail, miserably. She's not here. Honestly, she doesn't strike me as the type of person who would show up mid-game. If I had to put money on it, I'd say she's someone who is fifteen minutes early for everything, which is the way things should be.

I try not to let the absence of Kelsey interfere with my game. I have a job to do, whether she's here or not. Besides, we shared two kisses. The second happened when I walked her to her door. There was no tongue action with either of them. I like to think there would've been more, if I didn't have to be at the field for a six a.m. workout.

The final horn sounds. Dumbfounded, I stand there and stare at the scoreboard. We've won, but I can't recall a single play or touchdown from the game. It's like I floated through the entire afternoon, musing about Kelsey, when I should've focused on my job.

Back in the locker room, I sit in front of my locker and wonder how I managed to play one of the most challenging and dangerous games out there but can't remember a damn thing about it. *Did I get hit?* I shake my head, knowing full well that if I got hit, the trainer would've checked me for a concussion. Coach doesn't mess around with brain injuries.

After taking my gear off and dumping my uniform in the laundry bin, I head to the shower. Jessie McAvoy is singing show tunes, while the rest of the guys tell him to shut up. His current favorite is *Hamilton*. The songs are catchy, and after seeing the traveling production, I learned a crap ton about the revolution. Had history been taught this way back in school, I would've paid more attention.

The hot water feels good on my sore muscles. Tomorrow is a rest, relaxation, and massage day. The highlight of my week. I'm going to spend some time formulating a plan on how to woo Kelsey. I like her and I like spending time with her. A relationship may not be in the cards for us, and honestly, I should probably not jump into one so soon after Maggie, but I want to hang out with her and show her around. Hell, I want to see her at the game, cheering me on. Even if we're only friends.

Except, I don't want to be just a friend to her. I enjoyed the chaste little kiss I gave her and definitely wanted to explore where kissing could lead us. Still do.

"Who has plans for tonight?" someone hollers out. I can't tell who, but it's probably one of the single guys looking to go downtown for the night. At best, he and whoever ends up going will find themselves in a sports bar, trying to hide who they are under ballcaps. A few of the others grumble about going home. Me, I say nothing. I'm tossing the idea of heading over to Kelsey's and being all nonchalant about the game. But then I think women might not like a man who's in your face and being forward. The dreaded "my mom said you had to play with me" line is very much the same when it comes to dating—no one wants to be forced to hang out with anyone. I sigh heavily and toss my wet towel into my locker where it lands with a dull thud. It doesn't have the same effect as throwing my helmet or shoes in there. Instead, it slides down until it's in a wet pile on top of my other stuff.

Westbury elbows me and nods toward the towel. "What's your issue?"

"I'm in a funk."

"Because his girlfriend didn't show up," Chase Montgomery says from two seats down.

"Maggie's in town?" Westbury asks quietly. He and his wife, Peyton, are, or were, friends with Maggie. The breakup wasn't meant to be a pick sides sort of thing, but that's how it ended up being. More so because she's moved away.

"Not Maggie," I tell him. "Besides, we broke up. It's over. Done."

"Who then?"

The image I have of Kelsey flashes in my mind and brings a smile to my face.

"Moore's in love with the chick he had to show around the other day," Montgomery adds. For emphasis, he slaps my bare back with his wet towel. It stings like hell. I'd stand to kick his ass, but naked guys fighting is never a sight anyone wants to see.

"Grow up, Montgomery," I tell him before I slip a shirt over my head.

"You like her?" Westbury asks and I nod.

"We clicked. She's fun to hang out with. I took her out to dinner the other night and invited her to the game, but she didn't show."

"She say why?"

My head shakes slowly. "Nah. I think I sort of left in the air, ya know? I didn't ask her, no really. I was like, 'hey you should come to the game. There'll be a ticket for you at will call.' And then I sent over a bunch of gear."

"One ticket?"

"Yeah, I know. That's where I fucked up, I realize that now. I should've left her two so she could bring a friend."

"You should introduce her to Autumn," Julius Cunningham, our wide receiver, says. Autumn is his wife and our local weather person. She doesn't miss a home game. She's also a mom and brings their two older children to all the games. I'm not sure Kelsey would want to hang out with her. Not that I'm saying this to Julius. Autumn's great, everyone loves her. But not everyone loves kids.

"I doubt she wants to hang out with the wives," Westbury says to Cunningham. He then turns back to me. "If you're going to invite her to a game, give her an on-field pass and at least let her chill with Myles. I heard they hit it off. Don't throw her to the wolves before she has a chance to get to know them."

"See, I knew I messed up."

"You didn't mess up. You're just used to Maggie."

Noah's right. Maggie used my games as a way to network with sponsors and whoever had suites. Anything she could do to raise money for the children. I never faulted her for using the ticket I left her to increase funding for her programs. In hindsight, it feels like she used me.

Noah stands and starts dressing. I do the same, now eager to get the hell out of here. "You should call her."

I grimace at the idea but he's right. I *should* call, or at least text her. "I don't even know what to say."

Cameron Simmons, our cornerback, comes up behind me and puts his arm around my shoulders. He's the Romeo of our team. "Do you want my opinion?"

"Nope. But you're going to give it to me, aren't you?"

"Of course, I am. What kind of friend would I be if I didn't?"

"What should I do, Cam?" I ask, sighing heavily.

"Go to her work tomorrow."

"What? No way."

"Yes, way," he says. "Calling and texting is too impersonal. You helped her with this work thing, now go there, pretend you're in the area, and help her again."

The guys around me are silent and then each of them

mutters in agreement with Cameron. I don't want to admit that he's right, but damn it, his idea is brilliant.

"Fine," I say with as much exaggeration as I can. "I suppose I can be in the area."

Simmons laughs. "Atta boy. Be sure to let me know if my plan works." He walks away laughing. Something tells me if I fail at this, he'll never let me live it down.

## SEVEN

## KELSEY

This morning, on my way to work, I stop at one of the cafés I pass by daily. I'm not the type of person who splurges because, let's be honest, editors aren't pulling in the big bucks, but sometimes it's nice to be a little indulgent. I'm not ashamed to admit I live on a budget. It's necessary to watch what I spend. My biggest expenditure right now is my apartment. It's a little over my budget, but it's close to work as well as the grocery store and any entertainment I might want to treat myself to.

Today, I've decided to try one of these amazing chocolate croissants I've heard about from my coworkers. As soon as I'm at the door I see Russ Curry, someone who works with me, is there.

"Good morning," he says as he opens the door. "Fancy meeting you here." Russ heads up the non-fiction department and is always telling us about the outlandish stories he receives. He's the one who raves about this place.

"Morning," I say in return, and walk ahead of him. "Can I get your coffee this morning?" I ask, knowing he won't take me up on the offer. Russ is old-fashioned. At least, that's what he tells us all in the office. He is about twenty years older than most of us, divorced, and doesn't have any children. Russ never leaves the office before five and is normally the first one in. Basha has told me he's always invited to join the team at after-work drinks, but rarely meets up with anyone outside of work.

"Of course not," he says with a chuckle. "But I'll happily get your breakfast."

"You don't have to do that, Russ."

He smiles kindly. "I'm fully aware, but I insist."

I nod because there's no point in arguing with him. The last thing I want to do is hurt his feelings or make it seem like I don't care or appreciate his gesture. We stand in line for an excess of ten minutes and then wait just as long while our order is made.

"I normally order ahead," he tells me while we stand off to the side and wait for the barista to yell out our names. "But I was running late this morning."

"Everything okay?"

He nods. "I watched the game yesterday and put off the edit I wanted to finish. I ended up going to bed late."

"What game?"

"The Pioneers. They played yesterday."

*Oh, crap.*

"Oh, no." Dread fills my heart.

"What's wrong?"

"Nothing," I say as I shake my head. I messed up, but Russ doesn't need to know about my blunder. Finally, we hear our names, grab our coffee and croissants, and head out the door. My thoughts are on Alex and how he invited me to his game. I had every intention of going. But I thought the game was *this* coming Sunday and not yesterday. This could explain why I didn't hear from him yesterday.

*You also didn't text him.*

I like Alex. And the past few days with him have been fun. He shocked me when he kissed me over dessert, and again when he walked me to my door. I think he wanted to come in, but I'm hesitant to get involved with him after everything I've read online. It's refreshing that Alex doesn't bad mouth his ex. But it also makes me wonder if they're truly done with each other.

Russ and I make small talk on our way to work, mostly about upcoming projects and the weather. Unlike the dreariness of last week, this week is beautiful. The sun shines, and while still chilly, it's a pleasant reprieve from the gray skies.

Inside, and after a quick elevator ride, I head to the breakroom to put my lunch away. At my desk, I sit down and wait for my emails to load. I spent my weekend editing the football manuscript and left myself a bunch of notes—things I need to ask Alex. Of course, now that I stood him up, he may not be willing to talk to me about anything. I hope I'm wrong though.

It's almost lunchtime when Robin Boyce, our front-end receptionist, calls me. The dim ringing of my phone catches me off guard. No one has our numbers, again because of the open-concept layout. It's impossible to talk on the phone without disrupting people, and we prefer to do business via email. Leaving a paper trail is necessary, especially for negotiations.

"Hello?" I cover the receiver and mouth with my hand to muffle my voice.

"Hi, Kelsey. There's a Mr. Moore here to see you." Robin is incredibly formal and takes her job seriously. According to her, she wants people who visit (which isn't often) to respect Willamette Publishing, and by asking their last name, it shows they're respecting each other.

"Oh . . . um," I stammer, trying to come up with the right words. "I'll be out there in a minute." After hanging up, I take a couple of deep breaths and run through any scenario that might bring him here. I know for a fact we don't have a lunch date or meeting, and I was only just thinking about reaching out to discuss some questions—and apologize for not attending the game.

On my way to the front, I brush any lint off my clothes and try not to fidget. Alex makes me nervous, and it's because I like him.

Alex's presence catches me off guard. He's a looming feature in our small foyer. His back is facing me, which gives me a long moment to take him in. He's not dressed as I would expect for a usual Monday afternoon and is wearing slacks and a peacoat. In my mind, I see him in joggers or those tight pants he wears for the game. Although, the thought of him walking around town in those pants is utterly ridiculous. Still, the images make me chuckle.

He hears me approach and turns. The smile he gives me lights up his entire face and makes my heart beat faster. "Kelsey." Alex steps toward me, but before I can say anything, my entire team of coworkers flock the entryway.

The chorus of "Oh my Gods," and "Dude, you're Alex Moore," (as if he didn't know who he was) fills the room. Before I can even register what's happening, Alex is posing for selfies, signing autographs, and talking football with Jonathan. Honestly, I'm surprised at how fangirlish the owner is being right now.

"Wow, he's handsome," Basha says next to me. She holds her phone up for me to see the picture she took with

Alex. "You never see them dressed up like this, at least in person."

"No, how do you see 'them' dressed?" I emphasize "them" even though I know she's talking about football players or maybe even all our local athletes.

"In tight pants, usually bent over."

"Basha!"

She shrugs. "It's the truth. Didn't you watch any of the games yesterday?"

I shake my head. "No, I forgot." It's a lame excuse, but the truth.

"We should go to a game," she says, and I agree. "They're a lot of fun, and last year the team won the Super Bowl."

"The what?"

Basha's eyes widen. "Honey, you need to spend some serious sports time with that man right there. By the looks of it, he brought you lunch." She motions toward the small sofa near Alex where a bag sits. "Ask him about the Super Bowl. If anything, for research purposes."

When the last of our small staff finishes with Alex, he makes his way toward me with the brown paper bag in his hand. I want to give him a hug, but not in front of everyone. "Hi," I say, instead.

"Hey. I'm not bothering you, am I?" he asks in the softest voice. "I brought you lunch, unless you've already eaten, in which case I've brought you dinner." For being this big football player, he's a teddy bear on the inside. It's like there are two versions of Alex Moore. The person I see and have spent time with, and the person the public sees playing football on the pitch. They're not one and the same.

"You're not. I am surprised though."

Alex grins. "Sometimes it's better to see people than talk on the phone. Or text."

He's right. I'd much rather see him.

"Well, your timing is impeccable. It's lunchtime and I'm starving." He doesn't need to know I brought my lunch with me this morning. But that's fine, it will keep until tomorrow. "After we eat, I'll give you a tour," I tell him as we make our way into one of the conference rooms. Once he enters, I shut and lock the door, giving us as much privacy as possible. The last thing I want is one of my sports-crazed coworkers peeking their heads in with some mundane office stuff, which can clearly wait until Alex leaves.

Alex unpacks the containers and sets everything out. "Are you good with water?"

"I am."

I sit down next to him and lift the lid. The smell of bacon, cheese, and burgers takes over the room. It's not my go-to meal but I haven't had a good greasy burger in a long time. It's like Alex knew because now I'm craving one.

"I hope this is okay."

"It's very okay," I tell him as I cut the sandwich in half. "I can't remember the last time I had a burger like this."

"Yeah," he says with a sigh. "I don't do the frou-frou shit. Sorry." He shrugs.

I take a bite. As soon as the flavors touch my tongue, my eyes close. "Damn, this is so good." Forcing myself to put the burger down, I say, "I don't do the frou-frou stuff either. It's too expensive. I mostly watch my portions."

"Is that why you cut it in half?" he nods toward my meal.

"Yeah. Plus, I don't need to be in a food coma for the rest of the day."

Alex laughs. "I hadn't thought of that."

We sit in comfortable silence, and we eat the rest of our meal. When I finish, I wipe my hands and mouth and take a drink from the bottled water Alex brought. "I want to apologize for yesterday."

"Yesterday?" he questions. I think it's cute how he's pretending not to remember. Very admirable of him to not embarrass me.

"I had every intention of coming to your game."

"Oh yeah, that."

"Truth is, I forgot. I didn't realize the tickets you sent were for yesterday. Unfortunately, I'm so used to being home and immersed in whatever it is I'm working on that I space on things unless they're on my calendar. Even then, I have to set multiple alarms to remind me of things I need to do. After the other night, particularly the goodbye kiss, I guess I forgot to put the game in my phone. I can come this Sunday though."

Alex laughs and I love the sound of his husky voice reverberating through laughter. "We're away this weekend, but maybe next weekend?"

"Oh, okay." I don't know why, but I feel let down.

"You can watch us on television, even though I know you've never watched a game in your life."

"How would I do that?" Gosh, I feel like a boob not knowing the basics of how to watch his game on TV.

Alex reaches for my hand. "If it's okay with you, I can come by on Friday and download the app for you and show you have to navigate to our game."

"I feel like—"

"Someone who doesn't watch sports," he finishes for me. I'm grateful he interjected before I would have called myself something a lot more derogatory.

"I'd like that."

Alex finishes his lunch, and then we clean up. "Would you like a tour?"

"I'd love one." He follows me into our open-plan space. I formally introduce him to everyone and then finish at my workspace. "It's empty."

"What are you talking about? I have my laptop, a plant, my phone, and that stack of paper in the corner are the manuscripts or proposals I've read."

"And those books?" Alex asks about the two-tiered shelf under my window.

"Those are the published books I've edited. I get a copy from the printer before they send a box to the author or bookstore."

Alex goes to the shelf, picks one up, and thumbs through it. "This is incredibly cool."

"Thanks. I like my job."

"You really must love reading."

I shrug. "I do, but I love helping create a world where a reader can get lost. Many people use reading as an escape from reality. It's nice when you can get lost in a book."

"Do you ever have time to read for pleasure?"

"I do. In between edits, I'll read. What about you? From everything I've learned, you're busy."

Alex nods and sets the book back on the shelf. "Once the season is over, I'll read a memoir or a self-help book." He turns toward me. "I've been thinking. I was wondering if you'd be able to help me write a children's book."

"A children's book?" I ask.

"Yeah. Something I can hand out at charity events or when I visit the children's hospital. I want to write about football, but from a kid's point of view."

*He wants to write a children's book. And give it to kids.*

"Oh, Alex," I say as my hand covers my heart. "I'd love to help you."

The smile I'm beginning to love spreads across his face in elation. "I'm happy you said yes."

Did he think I'd say no?

There's a pause, neither of us knowing what to say, until he says, "I should let you get back to work."

I want to blurt out, "But when will I see you again?" as if we're starring in some cheesy drama. Instead, I ask, "What are you doing for dinner?"

"No plans," he tells me.

"Want to have dinner together? You can show me how to watch football. Six, my place?"

"I'll be there."

## EIGHT

## ALEX

For whatever reason, Kelsey makes me nervous. My palms sweat whenever she's near, and my heart races, like the anticipation of seeing her is going to send me into cardiac arrest. I don't ever remember feeling this way when I started dating Maggie. She was just . . . there.

Our relationship progressed slowly. At a snail's pace, according to her. We bought a house together, which we sold when she decided to move to London. Our breakup wasn't messy. We didn't fight or say mean things to each other. Our time together ran its course.

Except, she hurt me when she took the job in London. In the same breath, she opened my eyes to how stagnant we were as lovers. While we were good friends who were supportive of each other's careers and great for each other's images, our love life was somewhat lacking the excitement both of us craved. We'd friend-zoned ourselves without even realizing it.

I don't want to be Kelsey's friend or a *decent* lover, and I don't care if she's good for my image—although how could she not be? I want to be her boyfriend and the one who ravishes her body at night. Hell, any time of the day, to be honest. I love the idea of lying next to her in bed and just being there while she reads. I want to sit next to her on the couch and watch her red pen make annotations that make zero sense to me. When I look around my house, I imagine her here. She's on the couch, in the office working on a manuscript, lounging by the pool or setting up candles near the Jacuzzi tub. Her clothes are in my closet and her scent lingers in every room of my house.

But how do I tell her this after knowing her for days? The last thing I want to do is come off as someone who is looking for a rebound relationship because that's what it looks like to me. Until I saw her with Myles, I never believed in true love. Still not sure I do, but there's something between us and I want to explore it all.

I luck out and find parking along the curb. While Kelsey's neighborhood isn't great—not that much is in downtown these days—I'm confident in knowing no one will steal Rizzo. At least, if they try, it'll be a hard task. Rizzo is a chatty Cathy, thanks to some third-party apps, and if you touch her, she'll scream and call the police. It's a glorious thing, having a smart AI system.

When I get to Kelsey's building, her doorman acknowledges me. "Here to see Ms. Sloane?"

How awkward would it be if I wasn't?

"I am. I don't think I introduced myself before—Alex Moore."

"Yes, Mr. Moore. I'm a fan. I'm Barrett."

"Thank you, Barrett," I say as we shake hands. "I have a question. Ms. Sloane is new to town, and I'm concerned about security here." I look around and then back at him. Barrett nods. "How secure is the building? She gave me a code the last time I was here. Is it the same code for everyone?"

"The new owners of the building installed a state-of-the-art security system in each tenant's apartment. The code is autogenerated for each person."

"Good to know. I hated thinking everyone who entered could go everywhere."

"No, sir. They cannot."

"Thank you, Barrett. Have a good rest of your day."

"You too, Mr. Moore."

It's a huge relief knowing Kelsey is safe and makes me feel better knowing not every Tom, Dick, and Harry that comes in has an access code. Inside, I dial her number and wait for her to pick up.

"Hello," she says in a sweet, honey-toned voice. Sweet Jesus, one simple word from her and my knees knock together. I close my eyes and tell myself to get my shit together before I ask her to speak dirty to me over the phone. I'm definitely saving that moment for when I'm on an east coast road trip and pining away for her in my hotel room.

"H-hey, Kels." My voice breaks leaving me choice but to clear my throat. "Hey, it's me."

"Hi, Alex. The code is," she pauses and then rattles off the same four-digit number as before. "I'll see you in a minute."

"Yeah, you will." I'm not even sorry those words came out of my mouth. I desperately want to see her. Hell, I want to do a lot more but we're not there.

Yet.

It takes longer than a minute for the elevator to reach me, and then another two or more minutes for me to get to

Kelsey's floor. In the grand scheme of things, she probably knew it would take me this long.

When I'm within a few feet of her door, it swings open and she's there, in jeans and an off-the-shoulder sweatshirt that says, "Save the whales, trees, and the Oxford comma." I haven't a clue what an Oxford comma is, but I'm willing to find out.

Kelsey tilts her head toward the door. "Are you going to come in or—"

Her sweet voice brings me back to the here and now. I step in, cutting her sentence off. Kelsey shuts the door and before she can move past me, I reach for her. I've wanted to kiss her again ever since our dinner the other night. Tasting her mouth has been at the top of my to-do list.

My hand circles her waist, and I pull her to me. She emits a small gasp of surprise but her smile beams as our fingers intertwine. "I've wanted to kiss you all day," I tell her as I inch closer to her mouth.

"Me, too."

Kelsey closes the small gap between us. Her lips whisper against mine, teasing me. Or am I teasing her? My lips part lightly until the feel of her tongue presses against them. I open my mouth and welcome her in, letting go of her hand so I can cup her cheek, while my other hand pulls her closer.

We move together, in sync from the start. There's nothing awkward or unfamiliar about kissing her. This feels natural and perfect. Kelsey feels like home.

She moans and the semi I'm sporting rises to attention. I step back slightly, putting a little breathing room between us. She notices and pulls away. "I don't want to stop kissing you." The words tumble from my lips through jagged breaths.

"But you moved." The tone in her voice is sad and questioning.

I step back, clear my throat, and then look down at my joggers. I was a fool to wear them, but they're comfortable and unless it's important, I'm not dressing up. Not that coming to Kelsey's isn't important.

"Oh," she says quietly and then says the two lettered word a little more profoundly.

"Uh, yeah. Like I said, I really wanted to kiss you."

"If it helps, I feel the same," she says confidently. "I thought about you after you left my office. You were the only thing on my mind this afternoon."

"That's a relief," I say with a smile. The temptation to kiss her again is there, but I hold back. Hopping into bed with her seems like both the dumbest and smartest idea, and that confuses me. I don't want to rush anything, but damn it if I don't want to bury myself inside of her too. I'm on a teeter totter and I can't figure out if I want to be suspended up high or sitting on the ground. Something tells me being middle of the ground isn't going to suffice when it comes to Kelsey.

"Come on, I'll show you around."

Kelsey leads me down the hall. The first stop is the bathroom. It's small and decorated in navy blue, with a tub/shower combo, and I find the space oddly intimate. She shows me her living room again. The couch looks inviting and between it, the books, and her TV, I can see myself sitting there with her in my arms. Easily how I imagined us earlier.

Next is her galley kitchen. It's perfect for her, crowded for the two of us. She has a small balcony, enough to stand and enjoy a cup of coffee or look out, and a table for two in her dining area.

"This is where I do most of my work when I'm home," she says. She's certainly not the only one to eat dinner in front of the TV. "It's either here or on the couch, although sometimes I get lost in a good story if I'm sitting there and forget to edit."

"Understandable."

"Well, that's it," she says with a shrug and puts her hands in her pockets.

"Do you sleep on the couch?"

She shakes her head slowly and lets out a long, "No."

"Then show me your room."

Kelsey glances at the closed door behind me and then steps by me, but not before I can take her hand in mine. She glances down at our intertwined fingers and then continues. I get it, it's her bedroom and I just showed her what she does to me. Doesn't mean we have to do anything in there because the couch would suffice as well.

She opens the door to a bright and airy room. Everything is white, from her comforter to the curtains, to her metal bed frame. The pop of colors come from those decorative pillows people like to add in the morning, take off at night, and then add in the morning again, to the throw blanket folded at the end of her bed, and the three pieces of vibrant art on her wall.

"Who's the artist?"

"My grandmother," she says. "She painted these when I was a little girl and I told her I wanted them for when I had my own place. They were a housewarming gift when I moved into my first apartment."

"I'm not a big art follower so please don't take offense, but what are they?"

Kelsey laughs. "No offense taken. They're abstract," she tells me. "A bit of nothing and yet everything."

I stand there, staring at them and can completely understand what she means. The artist left the meaning of the paintings up to whoever looked at them. I turn around and walk toward her, she backs up until she's on her bed. I put my hands on either side of her and lean down to look into her eyes.

"Thank you for showing me around your apartment."

"It's small," she says quietly.

"But it's perfect. How about tomorrow, I will take you to my place?"

"I'd like that."

We head back into the living room, and I go to the bookcases. "Have you read all of these?"

Her eyes widen. "No, not even close. I keep a list on my phone. For every book I've read, I end up buying or getting ten. The cycle is endless."

"It's kind of like that for us players too," I tell her. "If they have a new product and they want your endorsement, they'll send you a sample. If you sign a deal with them, they send you products. Sometimes, they go overboard, but I get it. They want you to always carry their stuff around with you because they're paying you."

"Is that why you're always dressed in Nike?"

I nod. "I have an endorsement deal with them, plus they're local. The next time I head out to the compound, I'll take you with me. We can go shopping."

"Oh, new yoga pants. I like this idea a lot."

Kelsey and I laugh. "You're cute, you know that."

She blushes, the pink in her cheeks turns a lovely shade of red. "I don't know the last time someone called me cute was."

"I can use the other words if it helps. Beautiful, gorgeous, stunning."

"Stunning?" She looks at her clothes. "I've never been called stunning before."

"You are to me." I go to her and pull her into my arms. "And lovely, sweet, kind. You knock me off my feet."

"Is that a good thing?"

"Everything about you, Kelsey, is a good thing."

## NINE

## KELSEY

It's been two weeks since Alex visited me at work and then came to my apartment, and this weekend will mark the first time I get to see him play in person. And tonight, Alex's making me dinner.

At. His. House!

I'm not nervous. At least, this has been my mantra all day. Truth is, I'm scared shitless, and I don't know why. I like Alex and I know he likes me. If he doesn't . . . well, he has an odd way of *not* showing it.

We make out like horny teenagers, and I love it. I love every second we're together. We cuddle on my couch, watch movies together, and he's there when I'm working on manuscripts at night. We never talked about taking things slow, but it's exactly what we're doing, and it's working, despite my desire growing for him daily. I've never felt this connected to someone before.

The rideshare I'm in slows down and I peer out the window, hoping to catch a glimpse of Alex's house. Tall, still thick with foliage, the trees block the view of his home from the road. The driver turns and within seconds, everything opens and a white modern farmhouse with black accents looms before us.

"We're here," the driver says.

"Are you sure?"

"Yes, ma'am. This is the address you gave me."

My neck cranes, seeking any clue that this is Alex's place, and then I see his truck. A sigh of relief washes over me as I reach for the door handle. "Thank you." As soon as I'm out of the car, I conclude the ride on my app, and stand there, staring at the two-story home. "Why on earth does he need a home this big if it's just him?" I mutter aloud as the car pulls away.

Then it hits me.

*Maggie.*

They probably bought this home together, and now I feel like I don't belong. I look behind me, hoping to see the car, but it's gone. The front door opens and Alex steps out, leaning against one of the pillars on the porch with his ankles crossed.

"Are you going to stand in the driveway or come in?" he asks.

I nod, thinking I am going to stand here. I don't know what's come over me, but I feel like I shouldn't be here, which doesn't make sense. They've broken up, and as far as I know, they don't talk anymore. Of course, I've never asked him and have taken him at his word that things are over, and he's moved on.

Alex comes toward me and every muscle in my body screams at me to move, but I'm frozen. This feels entirely irrational on my part. He reaches for my hand, and then steps into my space, wrapping his arms around me.

"Are you okay?"

I nod, but the truth is, I'm not.

"What's wrong?" he asks.

"It's stupid. It's really stupid."

Alex leans back, keeping me in his embrace, and looks at me. The expression on his face tells me enough to know he's confused by my statement. "First off, never call yourself stupid. I don't ever want to hear you put yourself down again. Second, I can tell something's bothering you. What is it?"

"It's your house," I blurt out in the most ridiculous way possible.

He turns to look at his beautiful home and frowns. "What's wrong with it?"

"Nothing, yet my mind is saying it belongs to another woman."

"Except, it didn't," Alex says flatly. "Maggie never lived here. I bought it after she left. We had a house together, but when she decided to take the job in London, we put it on the market and I bought this place. It's always been just mine."

"For some reason that doesn't make me feel any better. Like I said—"

"Don't call yourself stupid," he warns. "Would it be better if we went to your place? I don't want you to be uncomfortable."

"No, I need to get over whatever this is."

"You sure?"

Nodding, I rest my head on his chest. "I have no idea where this fear is coming from."

"Me neither," he says as he rubs his hands up and down my arms. "Come on, I want to give you the tour."

Alex takes my bag and then my hand and leads me to

his home. It's gorgeous and I already know I'm going to love the inside before I even step onto the porch.

"I thought about putting two rocking chairs out there, but I have a great backyard space, which is where I spend most of my time," he tells me before we enter. The black double doors open to the entryway with a cathedral ceiling, and pine wide plank flooring. This is enough for me to know I'm already in love with his home.

The entryway leads to an open-concept space, with the dining space and kitchen off to the left, and island in the center with one side for sitting and eating and the other side for storage, and the living room off to the right.

Alex takes me to the kitchen. It's massive, with oversized cabinets, another island, and dual dishwashers.

"I know what you're thinking," he says as my finger trails along the marble countertop.

"I highly doubt it."

"Why does a single man need so much space?"

"Um, you're right."

Alex laughs. "My family comes here for Christmas, and I like to entertain. I love having people over and always want them to feel like this is their home as well."

*Better than the alternative floating in my head.*

"Do you have your team over often?"

He nods. "Especially in the off-season, for those that stay in town."

"Doesn't everyone live in the city?"

"No. Many keep homes elsewhere."

"I would've never thought that," I say as I wander around the island to the other side of the house. "Why do you have so much wine?" I ask as I stand in front of his wine cellar, even though it's in the living room.

"I don't know," he says. "My interior designer bought it all."

"Do you drink it?"

He shrugs. "When people come over."

Alex's couches are white leather with black and gray accent pillows. His fireplace is lit, making the room feel cozy. The space gives away to the outside, through sliding glass doors, where he has another fireplace blazing.

He takes me out there and shows me the bathhouse, except it's like a mini living space, with a refrigerator and snacks. It's a teenager's dream area.

"The pool's heated," he says as we walk toward it. "It's nice in the winter because you can swim whenever you want."

Back inside, he shows me his bedroom. His has exposed beams and leads to the backyard. "Do you skinny dip?"

"I do." He winks. "Maybe you'll join me?"

I shrug nonchalantly. I have to keep him on his toes somehow.

His master bathroom is bigger than my apartment. Until now, I used to think a big bathroom would be cold, yet his is anything but. I spend too long looking at the shower. There are three shower heads, plus one overhead.

"Do you use all of them?"

"Yes, especially after a rough game."

He takes me into his closet, which is where his washer and dryer are. Honestly, it's genius and there's no need to lug clothes from the bathroom or bedroom. Alex then takes me to the pantry, which again, is bigger than my apartment, and shows me the guest bedrooms which are upstairs, and then the downstairs media room, exercise space, and finally his office.

"I don't do much in here," he says as he opens the door.

"In fact, I think I've spent a total of ten hours in here since I bought the house."

"The view is so welcoming." The large windows look out over his well-manicured lawn.

"You can work in here . . . if you want. When you're here," he stammers.

"I might take you up on the offer."

Alex and I go into the kitchen where he pours me a glass of wine. "What's for dinner?" I ask.

"Take out," he says sheepishly and then shrugs. "I couldn't think of what to make and didn't have time to go to the store."

"Take out is fine."

He wraps his arms around my waist and kisses me softly. "I thought we could eat outside, and then maybe go for a swim."

"I didn't bring my swimsuit."

Alex kisses my neck, and then works his way toward my ear. "Your birthday suit will be perfect."

My body quivers and goose bumps spread out over my skin.

He notices and laughs softly against me. "See, even you agree."

"I guess I do."

While Alex calls for take out, I take our wine outside. Even though it's fall and there's a distinct chill in the air, the fireplace keeps his outside living space warm. Still, I shiver. Maybe because I know I should feel cold or because I'm about to strip myself bare in front of Alex.

I sense him before he sits down next to me. He rests his feet on his coffee table, pulls me close to him and sighs. "I'm glad you could come over."

"I should've made it happen earlier," I tell him. "You're always coming to my place."

"You live close to the stadium, it's easy for me."

"How come you don't live downtown?"

He shrugs. "I wanted a place where I could escape, where if I wanted to tinker in the garage I could. Or, run around naked. Sure, I have neighbors, but whatever. If they see my white ass running around, that's on them, not me."

I snort with laughter and cover my face in embarrassment. "Oh, God," I say as I try to calm down. "I'm so sorry for doing that."

"Don't be. I liked it. In fact, I like everything about you."

"That's refreshing."

"Is it?"

I nod. "I don't know what the incident in the driveway was." Shaking my head, I reach for my wine. "Nerves, maybe."

"I don't love her if that's what you're thinking."

"It is or was. I just thought . . ."

"I get it, sort of. But let me be perfectly honest with you, if I wasn't over my previous relationship, I wouldn't work so hard to see you."

"Like when you randomly showed up at my office?"

Alex laughs. "Honey, until I met you, I never wanted to write a damn book in my life. You're the excuse. The only one. I used the book thing as a ruse so you wouldn't see through me."

I think about the folder in my bag, filled with edits. "So, I've been editing for nothing?"

"No," he says as he readjusts to face me. "Once I asked for your help, I figured I better follow through. Now I'm excited by the prospect of publishing." He takes my wine from me and sets it on the table. "I like you, Kelsey. A lot."

"I like you too."

"And I know it's late notice, but I'm wondering if you'd like to accompany me to a fundraiser next week. It's black tie, and I can set you up with a personal shopper at Nordstrom's if you want to go."

"I want to go, but I don't need you to buy me things to try and convince me."

Alex cups my cheek. His thumb caresses my soft skin. "That's not why I offered. Besides, I *want* to buy you things, lavish you with gifts."

"I like gifts."

He smiles and blushes. "Well, once I start, it's unlikely that I'll stop. But in all seriousness, if you need a dress, please let me help. It's such short notice, I don't want you to stress." His thumb runs lazy circles on my leg.

"Alex . . ." my voice trails off.

"I want to pamper you," he says. "Please?"

Before I can answer, the doorbell chimes and he's off to answer the door. I use this free moment to walk over to the pool, curious about the temperature. I take my shoes off, and roll my pant legs up before stepping in. It feels like bath water, and I can definitely see why Alex skinny dips.

"Do you want to go swimming or eat dinner?" His voice startles me.

I turn and find him there standing inches away, this mountain of a man who I'm certain I'm falling for, taking his shirt off. I swallow hard and am taken by the intricate tattoo covering his pec. I thought the tattoo on his left arm stopped at some point, but that was probably because I hadn't seen him with his shirt off until now. I step out of the pool, coming face to face with him.

With no hesitation, my fingers trace the planes of his

pecs, down to his abs, and along the waistband of his joggers. "Okay, Alex. You win."

"This isn't a competition." His hands grip the edge of my sweater. He looks at me and I nod. In one motion, he pulls the piece of clothing up, and over my head. "Fucking beautiful."

Everything changes in this moment.

# TEN

## ALEX

Kelsey's fucking gorgeous. I don't know how else to explain what my eyes see when I look at her. She's a babe. A ten plus. She drives me crazy and just thinking about her makes me hard. Kelsey stands in front of me, in a white bra. There's nothing fancy about it, yet it's perfect. Knowing what's underneath the minimal covering has my fingers itching for a feel and my tongue begging for a taste.

My eyes go from hers to her breasts and back. The ping-pong match is dizzying, but I don't know where I want to look. Hell yes, I want to look into her eyes when I touch her for the first time, but damn it, I want to catch the moment her nipple pebbles too.

Kelsey's hands go behind her back and then the straps of her bra fall forward. I stand there, stunned, like a young man seeing titty for the first time. I know what to do. I know how to make her feel good. Except my moves are fuzzy. This is what she does to me—makes me forget—in a good way.

Finally, my hand cups her breast, and I swear my eyes

roll back in my head. Her mounds fit perfectly in my hand, as if they were made for me. I cup her other breast, massaging both of them until my thumbs graze her nipples lightly. Her breath catches and it's like a flip switches on in my mind.

Most of the time, I enjoy our height differences, until moments like this. I bend awkwardly and take one breast into my mouth, sucking and nipping at her flesh. Her fingers dig into my shoulder, her nails biting at my skin. I'm content here, until I feel her fingers push at my waist band and her hand . . .

"Holy fuck, Kels." My eyes definitely roll back as she grips my shaft, and it's my breath that catches when her thumb rubs over the tip of my cock. I'm hard within seconds and all thoughts of skinny dipping, dinner, and taking things slow with her are out the window. I pick her up, regretting the loss of her hand around my dick, and carry her toward my bedroom. She kisses me and rocks her hips against my erection. I've never been so thankful for my pants as I am now. Hers too. Because the way her hips are moving, I'd be inside of her by now.

Thankfully, I never shut the sliding glass door to my bedroom after the tour I gave Kelsey and walk easily into my room. I set her on my bed, and she falls gently with a plop and stares at me with lust-filled eyes. I step back and take her in, with her smoldering gaze, red pouty lips, and devilish grin.

"I have something to say before we cross this line. I'm not the player type that you read about, Kels. I don't fuck around on the woman I'm dating or frequent bars when I'm on road trips. That's not the type of man I am."

"Thank you for telling me." She leans back onto my bed, her dark hair splaying out along my comforter. Kelsey tilts her head toward me and then her fingers go to the button on her jeans. She's watching me watch her. I've never been so turned on in my life.

Kelsey shimmies out of her pants and pushes them off her ankles. I know I should've helped her, but I'm stock still in awe of her right now. First times are usually a clumsy mess of two people trying to get each other's clothes off, but not with her. She knows what she wants and has no qualms about showing me.

I push my joggers down and bend to take them off. I could've easily kicked them off but I'm afraid I'm going to stumble and fall flat on my ass. When I stand tall, she's seeing me in all my glory for the first time. My hand goes to my dick. I stroke myself, watching as she licks her lips.

"Come here," she says as she scoots to the middle of my bed. I want to do as she says but divert to my nightstand to grab a condom. I show it to her, and she nods. And then, I crawl to her, right between her legs.

Hovering over her, I kiss her with as much passion as I can muster and steady myself on one hand, while the other explores her body.

"I want to feel you," she says against my lips.

"Foreplay," I say in return.

She takes my hand and puts it on her sex. "No, now. Foreplay later. I want to feel you, Alex."

Those words are my undoing. I sit up and sheath my erection before lining myself up. I hesitate for a moment before entering. If she notices, she doesn't say anything, and I plan to make her forget.

THERE ARE things I should be doing. Warming up would be smart, but I'm anxious to see Kelsey. I dropped her off at her house before I had to report to the team hotel for the mandatory stay before our home game. Kelsey didn't understand why we had to do this until I explained the gamut of things that could go wrong on game day, and then it made sense to her. Still, leaving her after having her, was the hardest thing I've had to do in a long time.

All morning, I've been on edge, wondering if I planned Kelsey's first game perfectly. I made sure she had two tickets, and gear for her friend, and asked Myles to meet her out front to bring her into the stadium. So far, so good.

Of course, all my confidence might be from the high I'm still feeling from the other night. Remarkable is an understatement. We were perfect together.

Kelsey's walking toward me wearing jeans and the jersey I picked up for her. I have no shame, my name's on the back, and after our night together, I'm ecstatic knowing it's there. Her friend Basha is with her, along with Myles.

They're standing near the wall. Far enough out of reach, but still close that I can see her and hear what they're talking about. Well mostly. I pick up bits and pieces over the loud chatter of my teammates and laugh when I hear "men," "tight pants," and "bending over." We make eye contact. She smiles and gives me a knowing look. Similar to the one she gave me last night when I had her bent over the side of my couch.

Memories of last night flood my mind. Kelsey. Me.

Heads fallen back, sweat beading down our torsos. Names said over and over as we gave ourselves to one another.

*Great, now I'm hard again.*

Myles finally lets me have my girlfriend . . . the word gives me pause. Does Kelsey want the label? Fuck, I want it, and I think it's evident to anyone paying attention. She's down on the field, wearing my jersey, and I'm tempted to kiss her in front of everyone.

Except, I don't. With so many cameras around us, I treat her like I treat any other fan who comes onto the field —at arm's length. No one needs to know we are anything more. They'll speculate and post things about us dating. The media can spin and stew for a bit. At least until the fundraiser. Then, everyone will see the beauty on my arm.

I watch Myles take her to her seat, and then turn my focus to the game. For the next hour plus my attention needs to be on the field and with my teammates. Not on the hottie in the stands.

We take the field first. I amble out there, along the side of Noah, and we huddle up with the rest of our offensive crew. He calls the play, and we clap. I'm the first one out of the huddle and to the line of scrimmage.

Before I crouch down, I wave at the two tackles, trying to psyche them out. I swear I hear one of them growl, but that could all be in my head. As soon as I'm at the line of scrimmage, Noah comes up behind me. He goes through his cadence and I listen for the snap count and finally send the ball into Noah's hands.

I keep my eye on the middle linebacker who charges toward me like a bull. When he's close enough, I block him from getting to Noah. This is where I keep my attention, on protecting my QB until I hear a whistle or know the play has moved down field and Noah's safe.

The crowd goes crazy, and I look at the Jumbo Tron to see that we've scored and most of the guys are dancing in the end zone.

"Fuck yes," I scream as the scoreboard changes to six and I make my way off the field. The urge to look into the stands is great, but I hold off. Mostly because I don't want to see that Kelsey isn't enjoying herself. Football games are a lot to take in, especially for a first timer.

We gain a twenty-point lead before the other team scores. It's a cushion, but never enough. If we're not careful, it can go away just as fast as it took us to get there.

Play after play, I tell my line where to go, what to do, and encourage them to block all incoming linemen. Are we always perfect?

No, we're not.

But we do our best and then some. And at the end of the game, we're victors.

Fireworks go off and when I get to the sideline for the last time, I finally give myself what I've wanted the entire game—Kelsey. She's standing there, with Myles and Basha, cheering her heart out. Not only for me, but my team as well. Kelsey notices me and gives me a little wave, and fuck me if those fingers don't turn me on. She's going to be the death of me eventually but at least I'll die happy.

After the game, Kelsey waits for me outside the locker room. There are other wives and girlfriends there, but she doesn't know any of them and I haven't had the chance to introduce her yet. When I come out, she's at the end of the hall, waiting. I expect to find a book or a phone in her hand, but she's just there, with her foot resting against the wall.

As soon as I'm next to her, I put my arm on the wall and pull her to my body, thankful I'm wider than her so I can block everyone from seeing me kiss her. At first, it's slow, with a little bit of hesitancy, until my tongue traces the outside of her bottom lip and then she opens for me.

"You taste good," I say after we break apart. "Sweet, like candy."

"It must be the lollipop."

Images of Kelsey sucking on a lollipop flash before me. They're amazing images but they come at the wrong time. I groan and rest my head on top of hers. I love the height difference between us. We're perfect together.

"Where's Basha?"

"She went home. She has a conference call with a client on the east coast and it's at, like, seven a.m."

"You editors keep odd hours." Kelsey tries to keep them as normal as possible, but I've figured out since we met that she's a night owl and will either stay up until three in the morning to read or will go to bed early and wake at the crack of dawn.

"When you have clients all over, in different time zones, you try to accommodate. Plus, I mostly read and edit when I'm at home. In the office, it's meetings, conference calls, and a ton of emails. Anyway, she went home."

"Noah and Peyton are having some people over to watch the late game. Do you want to go over there? You could get to know some of the other wives and girlfriends, so you can maybe sit with them in two weeks."

Kelsey nods. "That would be nice."

"A lot of them hang out during the week or they'll get together and plan different fundraisers or events for us."

"They sound busy."

"I don't want you to feel pressured or anything."

"I'm not," she says as she places her hand on my chest. "I want to meet them, hang out, and maybe they'll teach me about the sport."

A laugh escapes me. "When the season ends, we'll sit down and watch a game. I'll teach you everything you need to know."

"Deal."

Cameron Simmons passes by and pats my shoulder. "Nice game today."

"You too, man." He made some unbelievable stops today, which saved a couple of touchdowns. He's definitely a difference maker, and if it wasn't for him, the score would've been a lot closer than our twenty point victory.

"Come on." I motion toward the exit and take Kelsey's hand in mine. "We'll go over to the Westbury's for a bit and then head to my house, unless you need to go home."

"Maybe for some clothes. Otherwise, I'll need to come back to my place in the morning to get ready for work."

I glance at her as we walk out into the parking lot. "Right. What time do you have to be at work?"

"I'm usually there by nine. Our boss doesn't care as long as we are there when we have meetings and our work gets done."

"So, you could work from home?" I wink, hoping to convey how much I want to spend my day with her. Technically, I need to go in for "maintenance" on my body, but I could postpone that. I'd love nothing more than to wake up with her, eat breakfast, and see her in my house on a normal day.

Preferably while wearing my T-shirt.

We get to my truck, and I help her in. I never want her to figure out how to use the tire to hoist herself up because that's my job. I'll happily cup her ass and lift her into my truck until the cows come home. And being that we live in a city, there is never any fear of that happening.

## ELEVEN

**M**y nerves are frayed. Maybe even shot at this point. What Alex failed to mention on our drive over to Peyton and Noah Westbury's apartment is that Noah's parents are in town. I suppose one would say, "no big deal," but Noah (and Peyton) don't have your every day, run-of-the-mill parents. They're not like mine, who get up and go to work every morning and punch the proverbial time clock.

Like, Noah and Peyton's are famous.

Like, uber famous.

Like, I'm going to pee my pants when and if Liam Page talks to me.

Like, holy shiiiiit, my heart is beating so fast I feel faint.

Alex parks and the valet helps me out of his truck. The stern look on Alex's face sends a clear message and the young man whose job it is to help ducks his head and mutters an apology.

"That's mean," I tell Alex.

"It's just—"

I cut him off with a shake of my head. "Go tell that guy

you're sorry. He has a job to do, and he doesn't need meatheads like you bullying him."

Alex's mouth drops open and my eyebrow raises. "Feisty. I like it?" He kisses my forehead and then saunters over to the kid at the stand. Next thing I know, they're posing for selfies and Alex is signing something.

He motions for me to follow him into the lobby. "Meathead, huh?"

I shrug. "I read it in the story I made an offer on."

"Have you heard anything back?"

"It's a lot of back and forth between me, the agent, Kit, and Jonathan. They want more money, which is understandable, but with that comes a lot of responsibility. On both sides."

We approach a large, semi-round desk. Alex reaches over the counter and shakes the man's hand. "Hey, Bernard. We're heading up to the Westbury's. This is Kelsey Sloane."

This man doesn't look like a Bernard. To me, that name says kind, caring, and the statue of a man behind the desk looks anything but. His penetrating gaze speaks volumes. He isn't someone you mess with, and you definitely don't mess with the tenants in the building.

"Ms. Sloane." Bernard's voice is a deep booming baritone of sound. I feel like I'm being scolded. I swallow hard and nod. "Look here." He points to the camera sitting next to the monitor.

"Do I need to smile?"

"Only if you want to."

I smile or at least I think I do. Bernard doesn't exactly give me a countdown, and I'm nervous. He hands Alex a slip of paper and then goes back to working on his computer. I reach for Alex's hand while we wait for the elevator. But even his touch isn't enough to calm the jitters.

"Stop fidgeting." That's easy for Alex to say. He's familiar with everyone we're about to encounter. He's not meeting Liam Page. Maybe I'm not either, but knowing he'll be in the room . . . like, what?

"I can't help it."

"Why are you nervous?"

I give him my best, "are you kidding me?" look, staring blankly at him like he should know. He shakes his head and chuckles under his breath. The elevator door opens, but instead of stepping in, he tugs on my hand to follow him.

Alex and I walk down the hallway, although I feel like I'm shuffling my feet in an attempt to keep up. He pushes me into a small alcove. It's private and odd. Why is there a random alcove down the hallway of an apartment building?

"Take a deep breath." Alex's hands are on arms, near my shoulders. He squeezes the muscles there lightly. "Noah's my teammate. I hang out with him and Peyton a lot. Although, she scares me."

"What? Why?" I'm so confused. How can a man of his stature be scared of someone like Peyton. I've seen her, she looks harmless.

"She could break my career into pieces if she chose to."

"Really?"

Alex nods and his expression turns grim. "Yep. She has this uncanny ability to break down a game and expose a weakness you're not even aware of. Coach trusts everything she says."

"Huh."

Alex gives me a little shake. "So, are you good?"

I shake my head. "You've met a lot of famous people, right?"

He shrugs. "I guess."

"Right. You see, I haven't met anyone famous at all. In

fact, I have blinders on when it comes to celebrities. One could be standing next to me, and I'd have no idea. So, the fact that we're about to go to a gathering and a famous rockstar is going to be there—I'm freaking out a bit."

The realization strikes Alex instantly. His mouth drops open and then shuts. "Sorry, I forget sometimes."

My eyes widen and I give him my best, "duh," face. "You're used to it. I'm not."

"You must know famous authors?"

"Not really," I tell him. "Most authors are recluses. They prefer to stay behind their computers. And honestly, they're normal people. You wouldn't know someone's an author until you started talking to them. It's not like Stephen King wears a banner that says 'Hey, I wrote *IT*.' Your friend group is on TV all the time." And making sexy gyrating music videos. But I don't say that to Alex.

"Point taken. How can I make this easier?"

"Don't leave my side?"

"Never." Alex's hands drop. One rests on my waist, and the other on my thigh, near my ass. I step closer. Maybe *this* is what the alcove is for—secret rendezvous and whatnot. hoping the latter hand will move and touch me a bit and move my hands up his chest slowly. I love the feel of his well-defined muscles under my fingertips. I lick my lips in anticipation of us kissing.

"Kiss me," my words come out in a whisper.

"Stop tempting me," he says in an equally hushed sound. "When we get home. I promise."

He said when we get *home*. Not back to his house or to mine. The nervousness I already feel increases tenfold. I like Alex and I can't complain about the sex, but I'm nowhere near the level of commitment needed to call his house my home.

It's way too early in our relationship.

"Did I say something wrong?" he asks. I hadn't realized my expression or demeanor changed. I shake my head.

"No, not at all."

"I did," he says, reading me better than I expected. "It's the home comment. I get it, but believe me when I say, we can take this as slow as you want. My time is limited because we're in season, and there will be days when I can't see you. When I say home, it's either your place or mine because it's easier than getting technical."

*Well shit.*

"You're right. You just took me off guard. I apologize."

Alex kisses me. It's slow, heated, and full of promise. "We won't stay long," he says against my lips. "Because believe me, I want to get you *home.*" He steps back. "Come on, let's get upstairs."

*Cue the freakout.*

Alex holds my hand and walks us back to the elevator. Someone is getting off when he goes to press the button, making our wait time even less. Inside, he pushes in a code, much like the elevator to my place.

"I think this is the best security feature. I love that my building has it," Kelsey says as the doors close.

"Me too," he says. "I asked Barrett about it the other day. I wanted to make sure the codes were different each time otherwise it defeats the purpose."

I lean my head onto his shoulder. He checked up on me. I think that's sweet.

Alex is quiet for a couple of floors and then tells me to turn around. I do and my mouth drops open. "Holy . . ." When I stepped into the elevator I didn't realize the walls were glass until now.

"Yeah," he says as he stands behind me with his arms

around me. "The city view from here is spectacular and it keeps getting better the higher we go."

"New York is like this," I tell him. "We have some amazing architecture there. Portland reminds me of it."

"Do you miss it?"

I put my hands on his arms and shake my head. "No, I like Portland. A lot."

The elevator dings and Alex turns us around. Once again, I find myself standing there with my mouth open as if I'm trying to catch a fly. "Come on," he says in my ear and gives me a tiny push forward.

We step out into the foyer of the Westburys' apartment. Only, it's more like a penthouse. For some reason, I think it's a good idea to count the people milling around but stop after ten. This isn't some small get-together, it's a full-blown party with music playing in the background. I rise up onto my tiptoes to get a better look. At what, I have no idea, but I need to see. Subconsciously I think I'm looking for Liam, Harrison, or Jimmy. I never bothered to ask Alex if Peyton's parents were here. Probably because I'm hung up on knowing Noah's are.

"Alex!" A voice shouts. I look around until Noah approaches. I met him briefly on the day I met Alex, but it wasn't more than a handshake and he was off.

"Hey, man." Alex and Noah clasp hands and hug. "Noah, this is Kelsey Sloane, the one I told you about."

Noah shakes my hand and smiles. "It's nice to meet you. Alex won't shut up about you."

"Is that so?" I look from Noah to Alex. He winks and puts his arm around my waist. "Did he tell you he's writing a children's book about football?"

Alex freezes beside me as Noah's eyes go wide. He

covers his mouth and points at his friend. "No freaking way."

My man nods sheepishly. I didn't mean to embarrass him, but it seems that I have. "I'm sorry." I lean in and whisper. "I'm proud of you and thought you would've told them."

"That's super cool." Noah says after he's gathered himself. "Come on, let's introduce Kelsey to Peyton."

Alex takes my hand in his. He follows Noah, meandering through the people. After a handful of delays, where I'm introduced to other players and their wives or girlfriends, Noah finally reaches his wife. Without a care in the world, he kisses her in a way I would describe as something that should definitely happen behind closed doors.

"Did they just get married?" I ask Alex quietly. To me, it's a newlywed kiss or the kind you see when two people can't keep their hands off each other.

"No, they've been together for a while. I'll tell you more later."

"Babe, I don't know if you met Kelsey earlier, but I'd like to introduce you." Noah steps out of my line of sight and says to me, "Kelsey, this is my wife, Peyton."

Her hand comes toward me, and we shake. She's tiny, even shorter than me, and I don't understand why Alex is afraid of her. "Hello," she says. "Thank you for coming over."

"Thank you for having me."

"Myles told me you're an editor at Willamette Publishing. How do you like it?"

"I love my job," I tell her. "And I'm sorry, I don't really know what you do."

"I told you, she decides our fate," Alex says. "Ain't that right, P?"

Peyton squints her eyes and glares at Alex. "It's nothing like that," she says. "I analyze the game and help the players play to their potential."

"She busts our balls," Noah adds. Peyton looks at her husband and it's like I can see a stream of love moving from her to him and vice versa. I don't know if it's the way they stare at each other or what, but they're probably the most in-love couple I've ever met.

After meeting Peyton, Alex introduces me to Julius and Autumn, his wife. And once again, I find myself standing there with a gaping mouth.

"Are any of your friends not famous?"

Alex chuckles. "I don't know if being our local meteorologist qualifies as being famous."

"I say it does."

"Duly noted."

Alex takes me toward the balcony. "Close your mouth."

"What? Why?" We step outside and there he is. *They are.* Liam. Harrison. Jimmy "JD" Davis. All three are more perfect than their pictures. They're sitting at one end of the terrace, and no one is bothering them. Alex guides me to the opposite corner, away from the band. "I'm shell-shocked. I need to get over it."

"I get it," he says. "I think I'm just used to them being around. Liam was at the game."

"He was?"

Alex nods. "Noah's family doesn't miss a game. At least his dad doesn't. Even when they're on tour, his dad is in the stands every game, no matter where or when end up playing for the week."

"You know, I think I remember reading something

about Liam and his son. I guess I never put two and two together when I moved here."

"4225 West does a lot for the community here. Anytime we have a fundraiser, they come and perform."

"That's really nice of them."

Alex nods toward them, but now that more and more people have shown up, it's hard to see the guys. I'm shocked no one bothers them. No one hounds them for photos or autographs. "Liam sang the National Anthem at the Super Bowl last year. It was poignant because his son was one of the starting quarterbacks for the game. I think everyone cried."

"Where's Noah's mom?"

"If she came, she's probably inside."

"Just hearing you speak about them makes me miss my family. We're close. Sometimes I hate being so far away from them."

Alex reaches for my hand. "Maybe they'll come to visit soon."

"Yeah," I say, nodding. "Although it's a good thing my mom isn't here now, or she'd be over there talking to them." My head tilts toward the band. "She's obsessed."

"Sort of like her daughter." Alex chuckles.

"More like starstruck. This is all new to me. It's going to take some getting used to. Who on your team has a normal partner?"

"Normal?" Alex's eyebrow rises.

"You know, not famous or on TV or whatever."

"Um." He looks into the apartment and shrugs. "I'm not really sure. Chase's best friend is a local radio personality. Cameron is dating a mega popular influencer." Alex shrugs. "And I'm dating an acquisitions editor. I'd say everyone is normal."

"You know what I mean." I push his arm with my hand, only for him to grab it and bring it to his mouth. He kisses my knuckles and then leans forward to kiss me.

"You don't give yourself enough credit. I think you have a very cool job, and I love that you're helping me write a book. I feel lucky to be in your presence."

His words, they melt me. I've never been with someone who knows what to say, without me having to point it out. I return his kiss and whisper a thank you over his lips.

# TWELVE

## ALEX

This week of practice has been hellacious. Coach is in a foul mood and has been all week. Some two-bit-blogger-turned-reporter made some pretty heavy accusations about him, the way he coaches, and how we're not going to make it to the Super Bowl this year. That alone pissed the entire team off. Normally, we ignore reporters like this. Everyone has an opinion and they're entitled to express it.

However, when he wrote that Coach was mentally abusive to us, it took things a bit too far. Coach is anything but abusive and cussing at us isn't any different than other coaches out there. It happens. We're big kids, adults even, we can handle it. Hell, most of the time the camera catches all of us saying inappropriate things during the game. Doesn't make us bad people. It makes us human.

To add insult to injury, Noah's hurt. He won't come out and say it, but we all see him limping on and off the field. He goes out for every down on first team and refuses to step aside for his back-up, Gio Munoz. Three years ago, he was a top draft pick, who, for some reason fell off everyone's radar on draft day.

Except for Bud's. Coach gobbled him up. In doing so, Noah's been nervous. He hasn't confided in me or anything, but I see the stress on his face. His contract has one year left on his ten-year contract, and as far as I know, negotiations haven't started. Neither have mine because honestly, I'm waiting to see what Noah does. I'd rather go where he goes, although I'm being unrealistic. Most centers stay with one team their entire career. Our bodies don't necessarily take the beating the other positions do.

I head into the weight room to get my lifts in. Since meeting Kelsey, I've skirted this responsibility a bit. I've cut some workouts short so I could spend time with her or, as Jessie McAvoy says, "to woo her." Whatever the hell that means.

I haven't seen her much this week but will on Friday night for the fundraiser the Pioneers are expected to be at. It's a big event at the Children's Museum, and in all honesty, I shouldn't have invited Kelsey. Mostly because I'm nervous. Taking my new girlfriend to the place my former girlfriend used to run doesn't seem like the smartest thing to do. I fear the people who still work there, and are friends with Maggie, may say the wrong thing to Kelsey. Neither of them deserves to have anything said about either of them. Maggie and I ended. There's nothing more to it.

In the middle of my bench press, Noah comes over and swaps places with my spotter. "Where are you at?"

"Fifteen," I grunt and then put the bar back on the rack. "You up?"

Noah shakes his head. "Peyton sent me over."

"Fuck. What did I do now?"

Noah laughs. "Nothing football related. She wants to know if she can have Kelsey's number."

Instantly my suspicions rise and for no good reason. Peyton doesn't have a mean bone in her body, yet she scares the ever-loving shit out of me. "What for?"

"She wants to invite her out to lunch on Thursday. Her and Autumn have a standing reservation or something and Peyton would love Kelsey to join them."

"Well, that's nice of her."

"My wife is very nice," Noah says with a bit of humor. "She's very, very nice, if you know what I mean." He waggles his eyebrows at me.

"Gross."

Noah cackles. "Don't even. There's no way you haven't tapped that yet."

"*That* . . . isn't a tree," I tell him.

"I was trying to be PC."

"Nothing about this conversation is PC." I shake my head. "I don't know if I want to give anyone with the last name Westbury my girlfriend's number."

*Girlfriend.* Did I just call Kelsey my girlfriend?

I did and I like it.

I try to hide my smile, but I'm sure Noah sees it. Thankfully, he doesn't say anything. probably because he knows I can kick his ass.

Noah holds his hand to chest and acts as if I've broken his heart. "You know my wife can make your life hell."

"Low blow, Westbury."

He giggles and sets his hands under the bar to aid my lift. I do another rep of fifteen and then follow him to the locker room. On our way, we run into Myles and Peyton. She beams at her husband and even though they keep their

PDA to the bare minimum, he leans down and kisses her quickly.

"Did you ask him?" she asks her husband.

"Yes, he asked me," I say instead of waiting for Noah to confirm. "You know you could've asked me."

"Asked him what?" Myles looks at all of us. "I need to know."

"For Kelsey's number. Autumn and I want to take her to lunch," Peyton tells Myles.

He scoffs. "You should've asked me. I have it."

"You do?" I ask.

Myles shrugs. "Of course. I love Kelsey. She's a doll."

"She is," I say with a sigh. There's a moment of silence in the hall, with everyone staring at me. I shrug. "Whatever. Anyway, I'll give you her number or you can get it from Myles. But I want to check with her first. Is that okay?"

Peyton nods. "I expect nothing less, Alex." She rises up and kisses Noah again. "I'll see you later." As she and Myles pass by, Noah watches her until she's out of sight.

Inside the locker room, I find my phone in my pocket and send a text to Kelsey.

> Hey babe

> Peyton, Noah's wife, would like your number. She wants to invite you out for lunch.

I hit send and then think I probably shouldn't have given that away, but then Kelsey would probably ask why, and I'd have to come clean anyway.

KELSEY SLOANE

> I. AM. DEAD!

Please don't die. I'd miss you too much.

KELSEY SLOANE

Seriously though. Her dad is a DILF!

Well there goes my ego

KELSEY SLOANE

You're my FILF

FILF?

Wait I'm not sure I want to know.

KELSEY SLOANE

Hahahahahaha

Footballer I like to fuuuuuuuuuuuuuuu

You get it

No wait

Maybe CILF

No, I don't like it

PILF

PILF? CILF?

"What the fuck is a PILF? CILF?"

"What are you talking about?"

I shake my head, a smile still ghosting my lips. I can't tell him my girl thinks Peyton's dad is a DILF. That could have so many repercussions. Although, I know Noah knows how people feel about his dad and father-in-law. Hearing it from his teammates might be a different story, though.

"Nothing," I say while waiting for Kelsey to text back. "Just some crap Kels is saying."

"You like her a lot, don't you?"

I nod and turn toward where Noah sits in front of his locker. "I do, but I feel like shit is going to be complicated come Friday night. I shouldn't have invited her."

"Don't you think she would've been hurt? What if she saw pictures from the event and all the other dates?"

"That's the problem. What if Maggie's friends say something offhanded to her or me?"

"Shit is going to happen whether you try to avoid it or not. You and Maggie had a very public relationship. It stands to reason people are going to say something stupid."

"Did that ever happen with you and Peyton?"

Noah shakes his head. "Not really, but Peyton has been a fixture in my life forever. It's not like she was new to the media. If that makes sense."

"Yeah, it does." I look back at my phone and see the chat bubbles pop up. "I just hope it's not a total shit show this Friday."

KELSEY SLOANE

PILF – player I like to fu… CLIF – center I like to fu… I can keep going.

But yes, give her my number.

No need to keep going. I get what you're putting down EILF

KELSEY SLOANE

Clever!

SOMETIME AROUND SIX, I decide to drive to Kelsey's. Traffic's a bitch. Bumper-to-bumper congestion, with pedestrians not giving a shit whether someone hits them or not. I lose count of how many times I honk at someone for darting in front of Rizzo. People see my Tesla and they don't care. When they see my truck, they're scared.

Barrett isn't at the door when I finally get to the entrance to Kelsey's building. The new doorman stops me, which honestly pleases me, but after the traffic hell I just went through to get here, I'm not in the mood. I should've never gone home first, or at least made plans with her. As it is, I'm surprising her and she may not take too kindly to it.

"May I help you?" the man asks as he steps in front of me.

I take a deep calming breath and remind myself he's doing his job. "I'm here to see Kelsey Sloane." I give him her apartment number, which he verifies on his phone.

"Please use the phone by the wall to call up to her."

I go in and call her, knowing full well I should've done this before I made the rash decision to come over.

"Hello?"

"Hey, Kels."

"Alex?"

"Are you expecting someone else?" I ask jokingly.

"No. Just surprised. Do you want to come up?"

"Nah, I thought I'd stand in your lobby and chat with you over the phone. Maybe we can do some dirty talk. Give your neighbors a show."

"You boob. Here's the code."

She deserved that after asking if I wanted to come up. I'm thankful she likes to joke with me though. I half expect for her to have her door open, but it's not and I have to knock. "Kels, it's me."

"Coming."

"Not yet, you're not." I mumble under my breath. I have a sudden ache in my chest, knowing she's behind the door. It hits me then. That's why I miss her, like physically miss being in her presence. I'm not here because of sex, but because of her. It's like my body craves being in the same space as her. It's been weeks, and I shouldn't feel this way. It took me months of hanging out with Maggie before I felt anything for her.

The door opens and my God, Kelsey takes my breath away. I swallow hard, taking in the sight before me. She's wearing one of my T-shirts. Not as in mine from my house, but from the Pro Shop. It's oversized and has my face on it. Her legs are bare, and her hair is in one of those cute, I-don't-give-a-shit, buns.

"Damn it, Kels. What are you trying to do to me?" Instant hard-on. I don't even bother adjusting the growing tent in my sweats. She knows what she does to me.

She giggles and the sound goes right to my dick. "I've been editing since I came home from work."

"Like that?" I ask, pointing to her attire.

She nods. "Are you going to stand there or come in?"

"Oh, I'm going to come all right." I step in and kick the door closed. My hands cup her cheeks, and my mouth is on hers before the door latches. She grips my sweatshirt and pulls me even closer. How that is possible, I'll never know. We walk toward her living room until I think fuck it and pick her up. As soon as my hands go under her legs, I freeze.

"Babe?"

"Yeah?" She's out of breath and kissing my neck.

"You're not wearing any panties." My finger slips between her folds and into her sex.

"Yeah." Her breathing hitches and her hips flex. Fuck

me sideways. "God, this feels good." She uses my shoulders as leverage as she moves up and down.

"Don't you want the real thing?" I fucking want the real thing. I'm hard and my dick is jealous of my fingers right now.

My thumb brushes against her sensitive bud. She moans and her head falls back. When she bites her lower lip and looks at me, I about lose my shit in my pants.

"I like coming home to this side of Kelsey."

"You can thank the book I'm editing."

Everything in me freezes. "What?"

Kelsey's eyes open. "The book I'm reading. It's hot. Very sexy."

"So, this isn't for me?"

"It's all for you, Alex. You benefit from the words I've read. Believe me, this is a good thing." Her hand snakes between us and into my pants. My dick's a traitor. An attention-seeking asshole. As soon as her fingertips graze the tip, he's all, "play with me" despite the fact that I'm trying to be mad.

"If you don't want this side of me, just say so. Jack will take care of me."

"Who the fuck is Jack?"

"Jack Hammer. My dildo."

"Your what?" I can't believe what I'm hearing. "Why do you need one of those?"

Kelsey grips my erection with some pressure. "Because this"—she gives a nice, gentle tug—"isn't always available. Whether it's yours or someone else who wants to have sex with me. Right now, I prefer it be you. But if you're upset because a book turned me on, then Jack will do."

It takes me zero seconds to come to the right conclusion.

## THIRTEEN

## KELSEY

I'm falling for Alex. I think it was inevitable. He's kind, funny, sweet, and makes me feel like I'm the only one in his world that matters. Alex is a gentle giant. This beast of a man, with the softest heart. And until I met him, I never knew I liked to be manhandled. The way he makes me feel when his hands are on me . . . safe, secure, loved, and wanted. I'm sure from the outside, we look like the definition of opposites attract, and rightly so. He's twice the size of me and could easily throw me around like a ragdoll, but he'd never hurt me that way.

When he texted and told me Peyton wanted my number, I danced a little gig at my desk. My behavior is completely irrational, and I promised him I'd be on my best behavior. My poor mountain of a man probably thinks I'm going to embarrass him. I'm not. If anything, I'm the consummate professional.

Except where her dad is concerned.

Her mom is sooooo lucky.

Still, I would never say anything to Peyton. I'm sure

she's heard it all and doesn't need to hear it from me. Besides, I'd rather be her friend and feel accepted into the fold of Pioneer WAGs. Their acceptance is more important than any dumb fantasy I have about a drummer, who is old enough to be my dad. Shit, I don't even have daddy issues and here I am thinking about someone's dad.

I meet Peyton and Autumn at McCormick's on the water. Inside, I give my name to the hostess and tell her I'm meeting friends. It feels good to call them that, instead of colleagues or acquaintances. She tells me to follow her. I do, but each step is nerve-racking, even though I know it shouldn't be. I need to remember they're football wives, and I guess technically, I'm a football girlfriend.

*Right?*

I hate labels.

No, actually, I don't. Labels are great because they tell you where you stand with someone. Asking for the label or checking to see if you're on the same page as someone else is awkward. How do I say to Alex, "Am I your girlfriend or hook up buddy?" It would be nice to know, but then again, is it really that important?

*Sort of.*

Peyton sees me first and waves. I thank the hostess and make my way over to the table. Thankfully, it's not a booth because who would I sit next to? *Get a grip.*

"I'm so glad you could make it," Peyton says when I sit down.

"Hi, thank you for the lunch invite. I'm sorry I couldn't make it yesterday," I tell them.

"It's perfect, actually," Autumn says as we shake hands.

"Every day is perfect for you," Peyton says to her. "You're on vacation."

"It's not a vacation."

"I think I'm missing something," I say to them.

"I'm still on maternity leave," Autumn says. I don't mean to, but I look at her midsection and think there's no way she had a baby recently, and then I think she's one of those lucky moms who can afford to take a year off and stay home. Autumn picks up her phone and shows me a picture. "We've kept his birth a secret. No one other than family and a few friends know he's here."

"Congratulations. He's adorable. What's his name?"

"Julius Jr.," she says. "But we're calling him JJ" she flips to another photo. "These are our other two, Reggie and Roxy."

"Your family is beautiful. I promise not to say anything. Not that I know anyone to say anything to."

"All right, enough about your gorgeous family," Peyton says to Autumn. "I'm starved and we have appointments to keep."

I pick up the menu and start looking for something. "Thank you again for inviting me."

"That's Peyton," Autumn says. "She takes all us newbies under her wing. Seriously, if you need anything, ask her or me. We'll help you adjust. Some of the other wives . . . well they're not as nice and accommodating. Alex and Julius are good friends, and we'll end up hanging out a lot once the season's over. Noah and Peyton leave us and head to California." Autumn rolls her eyes and Peyton scoffs.

"Assuming Alex and I are still a thing." I sigh heavily.

Autumn looks from me to Peyton, and then says, "Alex isn't like the others. He wears his heart on his sleeve and loves wholly. If he brought you to the game, it's because he thinks you'll be in his life for a long time."

"Autumn!" Peyton's eyes widen. "Stop scaring her." She

puts her hand over mine. "Autumn and I didn't want you to have to traverse the fundraiser prep by yourself. There will be media at the event, and we feared Alex wouldn't have prepared you."

"Thank you. He promised to pamper me."

"He did good," Peyton says. "Okay, let's order. I'm starving."

The waitress hears Peyton and comes right over, and we place our orders. Once she's gone, Autumn folds her hands and puts them on the table.

"Peyton told me what you do for work. I have to say, that has to be the coolest job. You literally get paid to read."

"Cool? I don't know about that. You're on TV."

Autumn waves my comment away. "It's not as glamorous as it looks. The hours aren't amazing. I'm either up at three in the morning or going to bed at three in the morning."

"How will that work with a newborn?" I ask.

"I won't go back to work until the season's over, and then Julius will be home. We do have a nanny, but don't want to burden her with a newborn."

"Gotcha. Well, my job isn't all that glamorous either. The pay isn't great and sometimes I offer freelance services just to get ahead. I do get to read, and for the most part, the books are really good otherwise I wouldn't read them."

"What do you mean?" Peyton asks.

"Being an acquisitions editor means I get to pick and choose what I want to read. If the first three chapters don't wow me, I'm not continuing."

"Then what happens?" Autumn asks.

I shrug. "Email the agent and politely decline. It happens, but I try to give each submission my full attention, which is how I ended up at the Pioneers practice. I don't know crap about football, but Alex helped."

"Yeah, not all of us grow up like Peyton."

I glance at her. She's blushing and looking down at the table.

"Honestly, I don't know anything about any sport. So, I appreciate the Pioneers helping me out."

"The owners stress the importance of community," Peyton adds. "We're more than just a football team. We're a family."

AFTER LUNCH and an afternoon of pampering, I'm ready for Alex and this fundraiser. Despite Peyton and Autumn prepping me, I still have no idea what to expect. I know the night will be perfect because I'll be with Alex. The only downside is the Pioneers have an away game this weekend and they're leaving first thing tomorrow morning. Tonight is all I have with Alex until sometime on Monday or Tuesday, depending on my workload.

My intercom buzzes and I rush over to it. Before pressing the button, I take a deep breath and prepare for the shiver Alex's voice gives my body. "Hello?"

"Hey, Kels, it's me."

Every. Single. Time.

"I'll be right down."

"I'll be the one waiting."

We previously agreed that he'd wait for me downstairs so his car wouldn't be towed. I step into the heels that match my dress perfectly and make sure I have my house key and phone in my clutch. I don't know why I'm a bottle of nerves, but I'm shaking.

The elevator ride down moves painstakingly slow. When the doors open, I expect to find Alex waiting, but he's not there. I step out slowly and hear a low whistle followed by a growl.

"Holy shit. Wow."

I come toward him and see he's eyeing me from head to toe.

"Honey, purple is your color."

"Thank you, I love this dress." The strapless number has a high slit along my thigh and tapers at my waist. When I saw it on the rack, I thought no way. The slit scared me and thought it would show too much . . . of everything. But it's perfect and makes me feel sexy.

He reaches for my hands and then steps back a little. He lets out another low whistle. "Damn. How am I supposed to keep my hands off you?"

"Maybe you're not supposed to?" I shrug a little. "Besides, look at you. You dress up nicely, and aside from our first date and the day you came into my office, I haven't seen you wear anything but joggers, T-shirts, and sweatshirts."

Alex laughs. "Yeah, I know. I'll be better."

I place my hand on his cheek. "I like you the way you are."

He leans forward and kisses me. "There's more of those for later," he promises. Alex holds his arm out and I take it. Barrett holds the door for us and tells me I look beautiful. He then rushes to Alex's car and holds the door again.

"Thank you," I tell him as I get in.

The drive over to the hotel, where the fundraiser is, goes smoothly and the only traffic we encounter are the line of cars waiting for their passengers to get out. "Why are there people lined up?" I ask as we get closer to the front.

"This is a pretty big event for the museum. Lots of celebrities come out for it."

"Oh, that's nice of them."

"Mhm . . . they're here, you know."

"Who?" I ask as I look at Alex.

"The DILFs you're infatuated with," he says with a smirk.

On the inside, I'm giddy and nervous. Maybe tonight I can at least say hi. On the outside, I touch the back of neck and tangle my fingers in his hair. "I've moved on. I prefer CILFs."

Alex laughs and shakes his head. "As long as I'm the only center you know."

"Being as I didn't have a clue as to what a center was until I met you, you can bet your ass you're the only one."

"Phew," he says. "When we pull up, the valet is going to open your door. I'll come around and meet you."

"Are you going to mean mug this one too?"

Alex groans. "No, I won't, and I apologized."

"You did."

He leans over and kisses me, and then pulls forward. As soon as his door opens, camera flashes go off. This must be what the gals warned me about. The media is trying to get the money shot. My door opens, and Alex's hand is there for mine to grab.

"Fuck, you're sexy and beautiful," he says when I stand next to him. "Just hang onto my arm."

"Okay."

We take a few steps and then the sidewalk turns to carpet. Alex pauses for a moment and then we turn. On each side, red velvet ropes and gold pedestals keep the media back. They shout Alex's name as we walk toward the entrance. They ask who his date is, but he ignores them. I startle when a photographer crouches in front of us.

"He's with the venue. Smile."

I do as Alex says, and once the cameraman is done, we head toward the stairs. Inside, I feel like I can finally breathe. "Is it always like this?"

"No, only a couple times a year, if that. This event is a huge fundraiser and draws a big crowd. That's why there's media outside. Last year, Denzel Washington, Julia Roberts, Brad Pitt—they all came. I'm not sure who's on the guest list this year."

"How did the Pioneers get involved?"

"All part of the charitable foundation," he tells me.

We make our way into the grand ballroom. It looks exactly like something you'd see on television or the movies. There's a jazz band on the stage. The dance floor is open and surrounded by round tables, each marked with a number. Honestly, I feel like I'm at a reception.

"So, what is this exactly?"

"A fundraiser," he says. "Everyone in attendance has made a sizable contribution or they've added something to the silent auction."

"What did you do?"

"Both," he says. "I have a game-worn jersey up for auction, plus I donated. The Pioneers have tickets to this season's Super Bowl, signed balls, stuff like that."

"And the DILFs?" I need to know if I'm bidding on something.

Alex laughs. "I don't know. We can go to the auction room and look."

"No, it's okay."

"Sure, it is." He laughs and gives his name to a man at the door, who repeats it into his headset. A woman approaches and takes us to our table. Autumn and Julius are already seated, together with two other couples whose names I don't recognize.

"Alex!"

He turns in time for a woman to throw her arms around him. I step back to give them some room. Alex pries her off him and tries to put some distance between them but she doesn't take the hint.

"Hi, Estelle. It's nice to see you."

"I've missed you, Alex. How come you don't come around anymore?"

Alex and I make eye contact. If he's trying to tell me something, I'm missing it.

"Uh."

"I know. I know. Things don't need to be awkward though."

"Right. It was nice seeing you, Estelle."

"Let's sit and chat," she says as she reaches for the chair next to her.

"This isn't the time or place."

For whatever reason, she turns and looks at me with nothing but snobbery and disgust on her face. Honestly, I'm taken back by her demeanor. "Alex, who's this?"

"My girlfriend," he says, taking me completely off guard. I do my best to maintain my composure, but I know I'm failing.

"Huh?" She scoffs loudly. "Does Maggie know?"

Alex cocks his head slightly. "What does it matter if she does, Estelle? Maggie and I aren't together."

Estelle's head whips back to Alex. "You know you can never replace her."

"Not trying to, Estelle."

She steps toward me, shakes her head, and then walks away. I watch her until Alex touches my arm. "Ignore her."

"Um . . . I'm not sure I can. What?"

"Seriously, ignore her," Autumn adds. "I heard most of the conversation and saw the looks. She's a snake. Always trying to cause issues for people."

"Oh, okay." What the fuck just happened? I close my eyes and take a couple calming breaths. If Autumn says to ignore that woman, I should. But I can't help the anxiety creeping in or how fast my heart beats right now. The look she gave me . . . if they could kill I'd be begging for my life.

Alex leans into me and whispers, "She's friends with Maggie. A lot of people are. My guess is she saw us come in together and figured she'd make a stink. Please don't let her ruin our night."

I nod against him. "Okay."

He kisses me below my ear, and then my cheek and finally on my lips. When he pulls away, I look at him and ask, "Girlfriend, huh?"

A wide smile spreads across his face. "Yeah, girlfriend. Unless that's too antiquated for you and you prefer something else, like partner or companion. Personally, I like it and it doesn't leave any ambiguity."

"Alex, did you play in the thesaurus today?" I ask, laughing.

"Maybe." He kisses the tip of my nose. "What do you say? Can I be your boyfriend?"

"Oh, God, you two are cute. Julius, take notes," Autumn says as she jabs Julius in the ribs.

Alex and I laugh.

"Yeah, boyfriend has a nice sound to it."

"Thank God." He kisses me again, and then pulls my chair out for me. While I'm okay now, I am questioning the earlier interaction. Estelle seemed mighty pissed that Alex had moved on, which I don't get it all. Isn't that what people do when they break-up?

## FOURTEEN

## ALEX

**E**arly morning flights, after a long night, are no one's friend. Of course, when the Children's Museum fundraiser scheduled their event, they had no idea we would have an away game. Coach always gives us an out, if we want to, but no one takes it. We all know it makes him proud to see us there, as a team, enriching the lives of children in Portland and the surrounding suburbs.

Dropping Kelsey off at her apartment last night and having to leave her there was pure torture. More than anything I wanted to spend the night with her. To take my time undressing her. To make love to her until it was time to leave for my flight, but I knew if I went upstairs, I wouldn't make it back down in time. If I missed the flight, my ass would be grass, and disappointing my team isn't worth the way she makes me feel. Neither is the fine I'd get. I had to remind myself there will be plenty of time for us once the season's over.

The sound of the landing gear coming down wakes the entire team. The flight attendant turns on the overhead lights, and window shades start rising, letting in the sun.

"Shit, I can't believe I slept the entire flight," Julius says. He's sitting next to me.

The plane we fly on is a private 737 that's been modified for comfort with each seat similar to those you'd find in first class. It would be near impossible to seat over fifty big ass dudes on a commercial plane. Not to mention the coaching staff, team media, trainers, equipment managers, doctors, and other personnel. The list goes on and on. Only the coaches sit in first class, including Peyton. Their seats are four together, two across from each other with a table in the middle. Most of the time they work or watch game film while we're flying. We used to tease Noah that he was going to have to sit with the coaches, but he never has and none of us know if it was something Peyton said wouldn't happen or what.

As soon as the plane touches down, I power on my phone and toss it into my bag. It's going to take a couple of minutes for it to cycle through and download all my notifications. The last thing I want is to feel it vibrate in my hand constantly or start answering messages and having to swipe away at the other ones.

The plane finally comes to a stop close to where our bus is. It's still early on the East Coast and from here we'll go to practice, then to our hotel. We have strict rules in place—no going to the bar, hotel restaurant, or ordering room service. Our meals are all prepped for us, by someone employed by the Pioneers. They work with the hotel on what the team will eat.

While I'm at the stage in my career where I can have my own room, I often offer to share. I hate being lonely, and it's not going to hurt me to let someone sleep on the extra bed in my room. This year, I'm sharing with Riley Mitchell, the rookie center, aka my back-up in the event I need one. I won't ever need one, but that's beside the point.

The Pioneers travel staff is like a well-oiled machine. They work tirelessly during our away games to make sure we are well taken care of. By the time we're off the plane and boarding the charter bus, half our equipment and bags are already transferred, and as the last rookie boards, we're ready to head to the field.

I sit back, put my headphones over my ears, and pull my phone out of my bag. As soon as I tap my screen, dread fills my entire being. I have hundreds of notifications. Text messages from Kelsey, my mom, my sister, a ton of Maggie's friends, and Maggie—*WTF?*—as well as alerts and notifications from Instagram and TikTok. There are so many, I'm afraid to open my screen to see what in the hell is going on.

Except, I have no choice. I open Kelsey's first. She's the only one I really want to hear from anyway. The first message is a link to a series of photos taken of us last night. I save a few of them to my phone and keep thumbing through the images she sent. My smile from seeing us together starts to fade and then morphs into a sneer. Photos of me, with other women who are not Kelsey and who I didn't even communicate with, are on my screen. With each swipe, a new one shows. And then the icing on the cake is a slew of images of me kissing another woman. No, not just any woman, but Maggie. Maggie who wasn't even there, but the headline states otherwise.

I know I need to read and respond to the texts from Kelsey, but I also need to see what's being said online. I open the internet app on my phone and type my name into the tool bar, something I rarely do because I stopped caring about what people said about me a long time ago.

There's story after story about how I left my date at the table to rendezvous with Maggie. There are so many images of us together, in compromising situations. Someone clearly spent a good amount of time photoshopping Maggie and I together. She's on the other side of the country, for God's sake.

And even if she was at the fundraiser, I wouldn't have left Kelsey. At all.

*But does Kelsey know that?*

KELSEY SLOANE

So, yeah. I woke up to these in my email. Not sure how they got my email since it's private, but they did.

Hello?

Alex?

Are you seriously going to ignore me?

Well, you'll be happy to know they have my phone number as well. I've lost count of the numbers I've had to block.

Seriously, Alex?

Kels I've been flying and I turned my phone off during the flight so I could sleep. I don't know what to say other than I'm sorry I'm not there to make this better. I'm sorry someone did this to us.

I read, erase, and type again, and then finally send the text to her. Nothing I say is going to make this any better for her. I should've known something like this would happen. The way Estelle and some of Maggie's other friends acted last night should've been a sign. They were nasty to Kelsey, and for no reason. They seemed to have forgotten it was Maggie who left.

She left them.

She left me.

The breakup happened because she moved away. I wasn't going to fly back and forth or spend the off-season living in England. Going with her was never an option for me. Deep down I think she knew this, and both of us knew our relationship had run its course.

KELSEY SLOANE

Since when don't flights have WIFI?

Our flight does have WIFI. I turned my phone off so I could sleep.

The chat bubble comes up, and then disappears. I stare at my phone for a couple of minutes and then text her back as we pull into the stadium parking lot.

I'll call you when I get to the hotel and we can talk.

I ignore the rest of the texts, even though I'm curious what Maggie wants. The only thing I have to say to her is that she needs to get her friends under control because this kind of shit is unacceptable. Kelsey doesn't deserve to see fake fucking images of me and other women.

As soon as we get off the bus, I hear Noah mumble a long line of expletives.

"Dude, do you need some soap for that dirty mouth of yours?"

"No," he huffs. "Fucking douche."

I follow his gaze and my mouth drops open. Peyton is

being hugged by another guy and it's not a friendly hug, it's one of those where you can tell the huggers like each other.

"Who's that?"

"Kyle Zimmerman."

"QB?"

Noah nods.

"What's your beef with him?"

"He's the reason Peyton was in the car accident."

"Wait, what?"

"Yep, he was driving the car. He walked away with a broken leg and my wife . . . well, you know the extent of her injuries."

Noah's close friends know how they've struggled with infertility, which the doctors have said is because of the damage she sustained. He doesn't talk about it much, but I know he wants to have kids. A whole team of them if he had his choice.

"I thought he was in Chicago?"

"Traded to Carolina two weeks ago."

"Oh, shit."

"For the first time in my life, I wish I was an outside linebacker because it would be my mission to take him out."

Noah has an entire team of defensive men who would do anything for him. All he would have to do is ask. "You know—"

"No," he says sharply, cutting me off. "I'm not that type of player, and I'd never jeopardize someone else's career because of a vendetta I have against another player. That's not who I am. Besides, Peyton would never ever forgive me. They're friends and I have to accept it."

"That's tough." I watch as Peyton and Kyle continue their conversation, and it's clear there's an affection which is more than friends for one of them. "He likes her."

"I know. Thankfully, she loves me otherwise I'd have to go all alpha and piss on her leg or something."

"Gross. Lick her face, it'll stink less."

Noah cracks up. His laugh is loud enough that Peyton turns around and leaves Zimmerman there. It's totally shady that he just happened to be here when our bus pulled in.

Peyton comes to us. I don't care that she's my best friend's wife, she scares the crap out of me. Her calm demeanor is a front for the evil that lives in her pint-sized body.

"Hey," Noah says as nonchalantly as possible. I don't know if I could be him right now. I'd have to know what the fuck that dude was doing here during our practice time.

"You can ask," Peyton tells him. He shakes his head, leans down and kisses her.

"I love you, P."

I know I should be used to seeing them like this, but I feel like I'm in the middle of something I shouldn't be. I grab my bag and head toward the facility. Inside, Coach is yammering about something and tells us we have five minutes to get our asses onto the field. This, coupled with the anxiety I feel over the images isn't going to make for a very good walk through.

I'M FUCKING EXHAUSTED when we finally get to the hotel. Once I'm in my room, I flop onto the bed and sigh dramatically enough that Riley asks if I'm okay.

"Yeah," I tell him. "I gotta go downstairs and make a phone call though."

"Want me to leave?"

While that would be ideal, it was my choice to room with the kid and it would be unfair of me to ask him to leave because my life took a sudden turn.

"Nah, man. I appreciate it though." I pull my phone out of my bag and see that the notifications haven't stopped. "Jesus," I mutter on my way out the door. Instead of taking the elevator, I use the stairs, and head right outside. Thankfully, it's warm out, which is definitely a benefit of being on the southern side of the East Coast.

I put my earbuds in and then press Kelsey's name on my screen. It rings three times until she picks up. "Hello."

"Hey, Kels. It's me."

"So says the caller ID."

I shake my head and inhale. "None of that sassiness, okay? I didn't do anything wrong."

She breathes in. "I know. I'm sorry. The articles are worse now than this morning," she says. "I don't know why I keep looking, but I do. Some keep repeating the same story and using the same image of Maggie with an engagement ring on."

"It's not from me," I tell her. "I never proposed to her. You know this. I thought about it, but things changed, and looking back now, it would've been a mistake. I wasn't happy with her. Not like I am with you."

"We barely know each other," she says quietly.

"That's not how I feel, Kels. I know you spend your day reading romance, and all those happily ever afters might leave you jaded, but I have some big feelings for you. Sometimes, the media can be assholes, but most of the time they're cool. I honestly think this is all spearheaded by

Estelle. She has a lot of connections, and she clearly had an agenda last night."

"I didn't do anything to deserve this."

"None of us did. But it happens. You have to ignore it and not let anyone see that it bothers you. If they know they get to you, they'll be relentless."

"I'm not Maggie. Being in front of the camera isn't my job."

I pinch the bridge of my nose. "I'm not asking you to be Maggie. I want you to be you, Kelsey. I'm not trying to replace my ex nor am I asking you to be someone you're not."

"I know. This is just unexpected. I wasn't prepared."

"Neither was I. It'll get better."

"Promise?" she asks quietly.

How can I promise her something that I can't control the outcome of? "I promise," I tell her. "Because we'll be together."

We hang up and I finally read the other messages. My mom is curious about Kelsey, so I fill her in and tell her how much I like Kelsey and enjoy spending time with her. My sister, on the other hand, is concerned about Maggie. That is, until I tell her about Kelsey and how she's my girlfriend, and that I need her to be on my side with this.

When I get to Maggie's message, I read each one and don't feel the need to answer them until I get to the last.

MAGGIE GARDNER

Well since you haven't called, I'll just tell you here. I'm coming back. I've accepted a job as director of philanthropy at the hospital. Looks like we'll be spending time together again. Can't wait to see you. I miss you, Alex. I miss us. Xoxo

> Congratulations on the job, Maggie. I wish you the best. I'm with someone now and I'm happy. I need you to accept this and tell your friends to leave her alone.

I send the message and then send a message to Kelsey.

> I forgot to say thank you for the pics you sent of us. You looked so fucking gorgeous last night, and now I can look at you anytime I want. I'll see you on Monday when I'm back.

After I send the message, I turn my phone off. If anyone from the team needs me, they know where to find me. Everyone else can leave me alone for a few hours while I try and decompress this ridiculous situation and try to figure out a way to help Kelsey navigate this type of bullshit. The thing is, she shouldn't have to. I'm a professional athlete for Christ's sake. People like me are a dime a dozen. No one should care who I'm dating.

## FIFTEEN

## KELSEY

Birds chirp outside my window. It's a promise of a new day and I'm determined to forget all the crap that happened yesterday. After a cup of coffee, I sit down with one of my manuscripts and my red pen. I read each chapter first, and then go back and mark whatever changes I want to see or note any questions I might have, and then I move on. My process isn't for everyone, and I make sure agents tell their authors before we sign any contracts. There's nothing worse than finding out during a status check that the author is beside herself because she can't read my handwriting or doesn't know what the editing marks mean. The last thing I want is for any author to feel stressed when they receive their edits back from me.

A couple of hours and five chapters later, I'm on my way to meet Basha for lunch. We try to do this as often as possible. I step outside after saying hi to our weekend doorman and let the late fall sun wash over me. There's a chill in the air, and it smells like winter. Most people say you can't smell the seasons, but I disagree. Maybe it's in my head, but I'm going to continue to believe I can until someone proves me wrong.

The sidewalks are busy, and Sunday feels like a workday with the amount of people out and about. I pass by a bar, with signs for today's Pioneer game. They're in North Carolina, and if I didn't know Alex, I wouldn't make it a point to watch. But I want to see him on TV and plan to root for him from the privacy of my apartment, while working. Honestly, today is going to be a good day, with the exception of Alex being away.

I never imagined myself dating a professional athlete or anyone like Alex for that matter. I always thought my type would be a businessman or a lawyer, someone who wore a suit every day and carried a briefcase. Now that I've been with Alex, I know he's my type. The man makes everything sexy, whether it's his ridiculous joggers or the tuxedo he wore the other night.

I sigh, thinking about Friday night. I've done my best to put it out of my head, but the images from yesterday, which are all over the internet, have really messed up my psyche. Alex tells me he and Maggie are done, and I believe him. However, after seeing the images of them together, photoshopped or not, it's also easy to believe otherwise. Even when I know they're fake and not really of him.

Whoever put them together knew exactly how to capture and display them as the perfect couple. The photos are nothing like mine and Alex's. I look awkward and uncomfortable, and he looks like he's there in form, but not spirit.

The ones with him and Maggie—the fake ones—look unbelievably *real*. And they look like someone caught their clandestine affair. They look happy and in love, while Alex looks like he had to force himself to take me. Even though this isn't how I feel, it's what my eyes see, and I don't know how to change that.

When I get to the corner, I press the walk button and focus my attention on the other side of the street. There's a park, with kids running around. A few people jog along the path and hold their stride as they wait on the corner for the light to turn. Other's mill about, sitting on the benches I can see from where I stand.

"Hello," the man standing next to me says. My senses heighten with the stranger danger feelings kicking in.

I smile and return his greeting. I'm very much the type of person who wants to be nice to everyone because you never know what kind of day they're having. I smile at strangers if we make eye contact when we pass by each other. More often than not, the gesture isn't returned, but I don't care. It's not why I do it.

The next thing I know, the man has a camera pointed at me. "Are you and Alex Moore dating? Why were you with him the other night if Maggie Gardner was there? How do you feel about Alex and Maggie being together?"

My mouth opens to answer but then I close it and walk across the street. If I thought this would deter the man, I was wrong. He's hot on my heels, firing question after question at me, with no signs of giving up.

I want to run but fear I will trip and fall. He'd surely capture my stumble and splash it all over the numerous gossip sites I found yesterday. Who knew there were so many? I didn't, but one search of the internet and ten plus pages flooded my screen with content about the gala. One site alone posted over a hundred articles about the people in attendance. I read a few about Liam Page and his wife, and I wondered how she handled the notoriety that comes from being married to him.

There's no comparison though—the things that were posted about Alex and me, and those I read about Liam and his wife. Liam's this famous musician, and Alex is a pro athlete. Surely, they shouldn't be treated the same way when it comes to the media and popularity. And why does anyone care what Alex does?

"No comment." I finally find the courage to say the two words most people say when bombarded with questions, but this man doesn't give up and the questions continue in rapid-fire motion. How would anyone even begin to understand what in the hell he's saying if he doesn't pause and take a breath before he asks the next question?

I pick up my speed and hustle toward the restaurant where I'm meeting Basha. Once inside, I lean into the wall and catch my breath. What this was, wasn't normal. At least, that's what I tell myself. No one cares that much about who I am.

Basha waves when I enter the restaurant. I have my scarf removed and coat unbuttoned by the time I reach the table. "I need a drink," I tell her as I sit down.

"I just ordered coffee for us."

"No, something strong."

"Why? What's up?" she asks.

I recount my harrowing trip here and her eyes widen, her mouth drops open, and then when I'm done, there's a glint in her orbs that makes me question her insanity.

"You should write all this down. Start a blog."

"And what? Bring awareness of what it's like to go to a fundraiser with a professional football player?"

She shrugs. "You're right, let's start a podcast."

I throw my hands up in exasperation, which the waiter thinks are a signal for him, and the poor guy comes running over with a scared look on his face. "Sorry," I tell him after he frantically asks what he forgot. "Can I get a screwdriver?" It's been so long since I've had a cocktail in the early afternoon, I figure I might as well get some vitamin C while doing so.

"Of course. Are you ladies ready to order?"

"A few more minutes, please."

He nods and walks away.

"How was the fundraiser?" Basha asks.

"It was perfect, and Alex was hot and perfect. Geez, I need a thesaurus. It's funny how I'll tell an author to use another word or be more descriptive, and yet, here I am failing at it."

"It happens to the best of us."

"I'm frustrated and angry. And upset. Yesterday, I was so angry at Alex even though I know he had nothing to do with the images online. Yet, I felt like it was his fault. Which isn't fair to him at all. I texted the crap out of his phone, sending him snippy messages, when we could've easily chatted about on the phone or when he got home."

"Except it's not something that can wait if a journalist is chasing you down the street."

"For what? Let's be honest here, I have nothing to give them."

Basha shrugs, and the waiter is back with my drink. We place our order and wait for him to be out of earshot. "People like shiny and new."

"No, people hate change. They were a favorite couple and I feel like I'm intruding."

"I'll be honest, I knew who they were as a couple and was surprised when they broke up. They were local celebrities around here."

"Great." Except nothing feels great. I feel like I'm wasting my time in a relationship that is going to cause me more pain than anything. No one wants to spend their time wondering how they're stacking up to the competition. Regardless of Alex and Maggie being together, I'm an outsider and to everyone else, I'm intruding.

After we eat, we sit and discuss work. We talk about the upcoming writers conference in San Diego and wonder if we should go.

"I want to," I tell her. "Escaping some of this cold for a week would be nice."

"We have to decide so we can set up appointments for pitches."

"I think we should go and set up a spa day or something. I could use one."

"Well, let's tell Jonathan on Monday. I'm game. Do you think others want to go?"

I think for a minute and know Sibley would definitely want to join us. She's our suspense guru and is always on the hunt for something that keeps her on the edge of her seat.

"Definitely Sibley," Basha agrees. "I can't imagine many non-fic authors will attend, but you never know."

"Russ wouldn't go," I tell her. "He doesn't like to travel or be in large crowds."

"Oh, that's right, I forgot. Okay, well it's settled. Let's talk to Sib in the morning and see if she wants to go with us, and then we'll beg Jonathan."

Basha and I pay our bill and then head toward the exit. She grabs my arm and pulls me away from the door. "Look," she says, pointing out the window." Outside, there's a small group, five or six people, huddled around. Three of them have cameras around their necks, and one of them is the man who followed me here.

"Son of a donkey's ass," I mutter. She laughs and then quickly apologizes.

"You should call an Uber."

"Or I can ignore them?"

"You'd be safer in an Uber."

She's right, but they're a waste of money when I can easily walk. I pull my phone out and request a rideshare. The ETA is under five minutes. Basha waits with me.

"They're going to start as soon as I leave here."

"I'll distract them."

"How?" I ask.

She shrugs. "I'll dance or pretend like I know one of them."

I shake my head. "You don't have to do this for me."

"I don't mind. Besides, it might be fun."

The car pulls up and Basha heads outside to verify the license plate and then motions for me to make a run for it while she works to divert the group of people toward her. I feel ridiculous, but here I am running to a car with my head down, to avoid having my photo taken. And for what?

Nothing.

I shouldn't care.

Truth is, I don't. It's the invasive questions that I care about. If these people need to take my photo and watch my comings and goings, so be it. Just don't ask me how I feel about Alex. My feelings toward him are off-limits. I text Basha, thanking her for saving the day, and sit back for the three-minute car ride.

It's all for naught though because as soon as the driver pulls up to my curb, there's a man with a camera talking to the doorman. I don't think it's a passerby or some coincidence. He's waiting for me.

I get out of the car, keep my head down, and ignore him

calling my name. Thankfully, he doesn't get past the front door. I've never been so thankful for a secured apartment building in my life.

Once I'm back in the comfort of my apartment, I change into sweats, grab a glass of wine—because let's be honest I need it—and the manuscript I'm editing before sitting down on the couch and turning the game on. I rarely watch television, let alone sports, so I have Alex to thank for today's broadcast. If he hadn't left me a note on which channel to find the game on, I wouldn't have a clue.

During the National Anthem, the video pans over the players. They focus on Noah for a bit, before zooming past the rest of the Pioneers. I barely have time to spot Alex before the camera switches back to the singer.

Alex warned me that unless I'm paying attention, I won't see or hear much about him. His role, while important, isn't talked about often. Unless of course, he's messing up, which he says, rarely happens. If ever.

I still don't understand the game, but it's on in the background while I edit. I manage to finish another three chapters and then take a break to refill my glass of wine. It's then that I focus on the television for a moment. The Pioneers are losing, and the commentators are talking about the uncharacteristic errors Alex Moore committed during the game.

"Bert, it's the reason he's been benched."

*Wait, what?*

I move closer to my television and look at the number on the jersey. Sure enough, the guy in front of Noah, who is pointing at other players, isn't Alex. Immediately, I download a sports app to see what they're saying about Alex. If I thought the articles about us on Friday night were bad, these take the cake.

## SIXTEEN

ALEX

We lost the game because of me. I couldn't get out of my own head enough to feed Noah the ball. The one job I'm good at, and I couldn't do it. While Riley gets his reps in during practice, he hasn't seen the field since the preseason. Probably something Coach will change now that he knows I'm a total fuck up. I have never, in my years of playing, had a game like I did today. I've never let my team down in such a way they couldn't count on me. and I've never been benched.

I don't know what happened, whether it was the stupid articles, hearing how upset Kelsey was and feeling like she didn't trust me, or knowing Maggie planned to return to Portland. Whatever caused the spiral, I need to figure it out. I can't afford to hurt our chances of making the playoffs. The day after we won last year, we all decided we wanted to repeat, and we had the team to do it. If I can't do my part, I need to step aside.

I avoid everyone on the entire flight home. During the game, after Coach benched me, they'd pat me on the back or shoulder, tell me it's okay, even though none of this is. I'm not hurt. I'm not bleeding, and I definitely don't have any bones sticking through my skin. There's zero excuse for the way I played. I put everything in jeopardy, including Noah. He could've gotten seriously hurt, or more than he already is, because of me.

Worse, my friend lost to the man who hurt his wife.

That's probably icing on the cake for me. I knew how important this game was to Noah, and I blew it. I let my personal drama affect the game, which I've never done before.

Some of the girlfriends and wives, who didn't fly to watch the game, meet their significant others on the tarmac. You can tell who has been married the longest, because their wives usually stay in their cars where it's warm. It's the fairly new relationships where the couple acts like they haven't seen each other in months versus two or three days. It never crossed my mind to ask Kelsey to meet me here, but then again, why would I? Why? Because Maggie never came, even when I asked her. Even in the beginning, she never came to greet me. Her excuse never wavered—she had an early morning and would see me after work. I accepted it, each and every time, without question.

Right now, I want to see Kelsey and wished like hell she was outside waiting for me. I should've asked her to come, but something in my gut tells me she would've said no. Especially after this whole fiasco, which I need to try and fix. I like Kelsey. A lot. More than I expected, and I want to pursue a relationship with her. I don't want her to think I'm only with her for sex or I'm simply passing the time until someone better comes along.

To me, she's the best thing to walk into my life since I was drafted.

After getting my crap from the belly of the plane, I head to my truck, avoiding everyone.

Instead of going home, I go to Kelsey's. It's late, but I need to see her. I'm assuming—hoping—she wants to see me. Thankfully, there's parking across from her building, and the night security guard doesn't give me too much shit about going in. For the first time since I started coming here, I don't call her. I use the code she gave me for the elevator and patiently wait for it to arrive on her floor.

When I get to her door, I hold my fist up to knock, but hesitate. Undoubtedly, she's sleeping. We didn't talk after the game. I couldn't bring myself to look at my phone and read the disappointment in the texts from my family. They'd wonder what's up and I have no idea how to explain what's going on.

I knock lightly, conscious of Kelsey's neighbors and the late hour. Each rap on her door gets a bit louder until I hear her shuffling around. "Kels, it's me," I whisper into the crack between her door and the casing although I doubt she can hear me.

Except, I can hear her and know she's pressing against the door to look through her peephole. I swear I'm in some romance flick where I'm about to profess my undying love to her, for everyone on her floor to hear. I'm about to start apologizing until I hear her deadbolt slide out and the chain dangle. Slowly the doorknob turns, and my heart simultaneously starts to race and fall to the pit of my stomach.

"It's late, Alex." Kelsey only opens the door a sliver, not inviting me in. That feeling I had in my heart moments ago is definitely stronger than I expected or ever experienced. She doesn't want me here, and I don't blame her.

"I know. I'm sorry. I'll go." I turn to leave, but her voice stops me.

"No, wait." She opens the door and invites me in. The warmth of her apartment welcomes me. I inhale deeply and then let the air out of my lungs slowly. I turn at the sound of the locks engaging, and our eyes meet. The pain all this media shit caused her is clear. I step forward to cup her cheek, just as her hand turns to kiss my palm.

"I'm sorry," I whisper.

"It's okay."

"It's not." I shake my head. "None of this is okay."

Kelsey leans her head into my hand, but this isn't enough for me. I bring her to my chest and wrap my arms around her.

"It's late," she repeats from earlier.

"I'll go."

"No, stay." She takes my hand and leads me to her room. She waits for me to enter before shutting the door behind us. I strip down to my boxers and crawl in bed behind her.

"Come here." I hold my arms open and wait for her to move into my cocoon. As much as I want to be with her, holding her like this is far more important to me. I bury my nose in her hair and inhale the vanilla of her shampoo. "My little spoon."

Kelsey laughs and grips my arms with her hands. "I feel safe here."

I have no words. Nothing witty or sincere to say back to her. I want her to feel safe, and yet the rag gossip blogs, and wannabe journalists, made her feel less than safe. They made her question whether she belongs with me or not. It's unacceptable.

WHEN I WAKE, I'm alone in Kelsey's room. I can smell freshly brewed coffee coming from the kitchen and hear soft music playing. There's a bit of light peeking through her blinds, but it's muted. I listen hard for the distinct sound rain makes when hitting windows, and groan. I roll onto my back and stare at the white ceiling, and then onto my side, because the view is much better. I love the art on her walls —the paintings her grandmother created. And while Kelsey's room is white, it's soft and homey. I feel safe here.

I'd give anything for this to be a Saturday or Sunday, where we could stay in bed all day together, and not a Monday where she has to go to work. I have the rest of today to figure out my shit before I'm called into Coach's office. Tomorrow isn't going to be fun. Once he rips my ass, Peyton will do the same, although her way is in the evilest way possible. She never tells us we suck. She makes us watch game film, and when we commit an error, she pauses it and then glares at us. That pint-sized devil is mean. I can't imagine the dinner conversation after she's had meetings with Noah. But then again, he's married to her and I have no doubt he can sweet talk his way out of her villainous looks.

As much as I don't want to get out of bed, I do, and make my way into the other room, wearing just my boxers. "Morning," I say, rubbing my face and hair, and then finally my chest.

"Good morning. There's coffee in the pot," Kelsey says

as she looks me over. I can't tell if she's angry with me or not.

I return to the living room with the pot and refill her cup. "Can I get you anything else?"

"No, thanks."

After replacing the coffee pot in the kitchen, I walk back to the living room and sit facing her on the small coffee table. "About last night."

Kelsey laughs, and while normally I'd be okay with hearing this sound come from her, I'm not right now. I'm vulnerable, sitting here in my boxers.

"I'm sorry," she says, but continues to giggle. "That's a movie . . . about sex and romance."

"Well, I'm pretty good at one of those things." I waggle my eyebrows.

"Definitely," she says without elaborating. Yep, I get it, my romance skills need a little work. I could easily use the "I'm a football player" excuse, but the truth is, I don't romance well. It's a learned art, which there are no teachers for. It's not like us guys sit around in the locker room talking about how to romance our women. Shit, maybe I need to hang out with Noah more, or Julius. He had to woo the shit out of Autumn after he almost fucked that relationship up.

"Should I ask you to tell which one I'm good at?"

Kelsey blushes and the sight of her cheeks turning a beautiful shade of pink at my suggestiveness goes right to my groin. She must expect this reaction from me because her eyes dart toward my lap and then back to my face.

"Come sit on my lap," I say, in a throaty tone that's meant to be sexy.

Kelsey rises and saunters over to me. My hands reach out and rest on her hips, guiding her to me. As soon as she brushes against my growing hard-on, my eyes close and I groan. "Fuck, I want to be inside of you."

"We shouldn't."

*Because of work?*

*Because of the shit going on?*

My hands move up her back and I pull her to me for a deep kiss. She needs to feel how sorry I am for everything. "I'm sorry," I say again as my lips ghost over hers. "Tell me how to fix it."

Kelsey pulls away and looks at me with unshed tears in her eyes. "I'm going to be fine. Everything caught me off guard."

*She's going to be fine.*

"What about us?"

"Is there an us?" she asks.

I start to nod before she even finishes her question. "I want there to be. God, Kels, I'm head over heels for you and sick to my stomach people think this type of treatment's okay. It's not, but I also don't know how to fix it." I leave out the part where I asked Maggie to tell her friends to chill out. "I don't want some local news fodder to come between us." Short of begging her to stay with me, I don't know what else to do.

"I don't either."

I brush her hair off her shoulders. "Tell me what I can do."

"This is new territory for me. I've never dated anyone famous before."

I scoff so loudly, she startles. "I'm not famous, honey. I'm the center of a football team that just so happened to win the Super Bowl last year. Hell, until then, I don't think anyone knew my name. They referred to me as the guy who passed Noah Westbury the ball."

"You don't give yourself enough credit."

I sigh and kiss her pouty lips. "I know, but still. I don't feel famous. Maybe I'm used to it because I've lived the past few years with people always taking photos and videos of me. It's something I'm used to. But I'm by no means a 'celebrity.'"

"And it might be something I need to get used to, although I don't want to," she says. "I expect it when we're together, but when we're not, I don't want these people following me wherever I go."

"Understandable. I'll tell them to stop."

"You can do that?"

Shrugging, I look into her eyes. "I'm going to try. You're someone I want to spend a lot of time with, and if it means pissing off the journalists in the area, so be it. Although"—I lean forward and stand with her—"make up sex is really, really fun." Kelsey giggles into my shoulder as I take us into her room.

## SEVENTEEN

## KELSEY

We are going on to week four of the epic media meltdown. They've left me alone. They've left Alex alone. This is a relief. We are a couple, doing couple things when we're together. Over the past month, Alex has shown me Portland, the way only a local could. He's taken me to the Portland Saturday Market, which has quickly become my go-to place for shopping. As long as he's in town, we go out to breakfast every Saturday morning. I think my favorite has been our Monday nights. He picks me up and cooks us dinner. Most of the time we eat outside, by the fireplace. Both of us are trying to prolong fall as long as possible.

I never asked him about the game he didn't play in. The week after they came back from North Carolina was stressful for him. He didn't need me, someone who barely understands the game of football, to ask him why he had to sit out. I remembered everything the commentators said that day and that was enough for me to know it was bad. I also didn't bring it up because I feel like some of what happened to him is my fault. There wasn't a need for me to be so hard on him when he did nothing wrong.

Basha comes up to my desk with a shit-eating grin on her face. Lately, she's been extremely happy because one of her historical fiction novels debuted number one in the New York Times, and according to the agent on record, numerous producers are hot after the movie rights. When something like this happens, the publisher benefits greatly. For Basha, when she makes an offer on another book, she'll be able to throw this tidbit out during the early stages of negotiations. It's a win for everyone involved.

"You're up to something," I say to her as she hangs her arms over the wall of my cubicle.

"Your honey is a thirst trap."

I rue the day I told Basha about Alex calling me honey. I couldn't help myself. I've never been the type who needs a pet name, but when he says it, the sweet word drizzles in temptation. He makes me weak in my knees and then some.

Basha hands me her headphones and once I have them secured over my ears, she plays a video on her phone. It's a short clip of Alex, from different days, wearing pretty much the same thing: gray or dark gray sweats and a hoodie. He's either carrying a tray with two paper coffee cups on it or he's walking somewhere. If I had to guess, he's leaving my apartment. Once the video restarts, Basha presses the comments and points to them.

There's a smile on my face when I see comments like:

- Tiffanyregnier6: Alex Moore is my favorite human.
- littleimps35: Protect Alex at all costs.
- book_nerd13: How can you not like Alex Moore?

- sailinfish: I love it when Alex dances in the end zone.
- However, my eyes bug out of when I read things like:
- Leskurk19: Alex Moore is fine as wine and I'm a drinker.
- deelagasse: If his lady doesn't husband him up, I'm going to.
- demonaco_jade1231: Can Alex be any more adorable?
- wendyywu13: Alex Moore = sexy beast.
- amhaven_I neeeeeed Moore of Alex (y'all see what I did there?).
- MBurz716: Is Alex dating anyone because I'm single and ready to mingle.
- MelissaRose_4: My obsession!
- eliayon: I want to be a Noah-Alex sandwich.
- robin_a.k.a_kirst_kels_mom: Imagine being the ball that's passed between Alex's legs.

After the last one hitting a bit close to home with "Kels" I hand Basha her phone back. "I have no words."

"People are hot for your man."

"This is a good thing, right? Like I should be okay with internet strangers having a thing for him?"

Basha shrugs. "I've never been in the position you're in." She taps on her phone and then looks at me. "Are any of these comments true?"

I shrug and look away sheepishly. Alex *is* adorable. He *is* fine. But what they don't cover are things they don't know, like how when we're watching TV or reading, he always drapes my legs over his or how he fluffs my pillow before we go to bed.

The comment about me turning him into my husband, though, neither of us are there yet. He needs to move slow after his relationship with Maggie, and I fully understand and accept this decision. Besides, why rush?

Him being a sexy beast . . . yeah, I'm not admitting anything to Basha. I don't need her looking at him, especially when he shows up here in his daily attire, and wondering just how sexy he is under those clothes.

She turns her phone to me, showing me another video of Alex working out at the gym. He's shirtless and seems to be by himself. As far as I knew, he only works out at the practice facility, and I can't imagine any of the other guys filming their workouts.

"Where is this from?"

"His account."

"He has one?"

She nods and shows me the profile. I had no idea, but then again, it's not something we've talked about. I don't do much on social media, mostly because of time and I find my life to be extremely boring. No one cares what a book editor is up to every day. It would be the same mundane content, day after day. Coffee, work, books.

"Huh."

"You should download the app and look through his videos."

"Yeah, maybe. What's it called?"

Basha takes my phone from me and presses the screen. After a few minutes, she hands it back to me. "I gave you a screen name."

I freeze and am afraid to ask. "Wh-what's my name?"

"Nothing bad and very fitting."

"Uh, huh."

"Book Girl."

It's not bad. "Cute."

"You should see how long it takes for Alex to realize it's you." Basha laughs.

"Seems extremely deceitful."

I don't know why, but she has to think about what I said for a minute. "Okay, yeah. Just comment."

"I'll do it after our meeting." I've never been so excited for a meeting in my life. I'm not sure what went through Basha's mind a moment ago, but it makes me wonder if she thinks Alex isn't faithful to me. He's never given me a reason not to trust him, and I don't want to do something that could hurt our relationship. I'm tempted to delete the app. Except I want to look at his videos. I may have the real guy in my life but having these videos to look at is nice as well.

I'm about to leave my desk when I get an alert for a new email. I don't know what possesses me to look, but I do. A huge wave of relief washes over me when I see who it's from and the subject: OFFER ACCEPTED. I fist pump as I open and read that the author of the football romance has accepted the deal I put forth. I write back, letting the agent know I'll send over an offer sheet for her to sign, and then we'll get a full contract sent. All this tedious paperwork should be boilerplate, but it's not. It'll take our legal department weeks to generate the standard contract, and the agent will mark things they don't like, thus another round of back and forth begins.

I head into our meeting with the good news. Jonathan asks us each for a status update and Russ starts off with his current projects explaining he's a bit wary about a bombshell tell-all we're going to publish. "I'm reading content that makes me uncomfortable," he tells us. "I'm not sure what we should do."

"Is it going to harm the company?" Jonathan asks.

Russ thinks for a minute and slowly shakes his head. "No, but the media will have a field day with it."

"Which means more sales," Basha added. "And more publicity for us because celebs will see Willamette Publishing as a place to publish their tell-alls without criticism."

"Basha has a point," I say to the group. "If the content doesn't hurt us, who are we to say it shouldn't be published?"

"I see your point," Russ concedes. "I can't help but worry, sometimes."

"The worst that can happen is our name is out there," Jonathan says. "Okay, who's next?"

"I'll go," I say. "I just got word that the author of the football romance has accepted. I'm excited to work on this project."

"Well, at least if you have questions, you know where to go," Jonathan adds. "Make sure legal starts the paperwork sooner rather than later. Lord knows they take their sweet time. Okay, what else?"

Basha goes next, praising her author for her New York Times listing, and letting us know she's in final talks for two more books in the series.

Jonathan talks numbers, which I hate. Most of the time they don't make sense to me. I know what I can offer each author, and anything over the limit, Jonathan either approves or denies. Yet, each week, we go over the financials and it's like I'm underwater when he throws profit margins, losses, and some other fancy words out there. My thing is books. It's words on pages that take me away to some other place while reading. The money talk isn't for me.

After the meeting concludes, I head into the breakroom

and make myself a cup of coffee before heading back to my desk. I check my phone and find a couple text messages from Alex.

ALEX MOORE

Hey honey.

Honey?

Yo, girlfriend

Okay, I get it. You're busy.

The messages bring a smile to my face, and I quickly write back.

Sorry. Staff meeting. Guess what, the author for the football book—accepted!

ALEX MOORE

Ah, so you are using me for my knowledge of the sport!

I giggle, a bit louder than I should and type out my reply.

And your body!

ALEX MOORE

I knew it and honestly, I'm okay with it.

See you after work.

I just wanted to let you know I'm thinking about you.

As much as I want to reply, I'd end up texting with him all day. Such is the life of working a full-time, Monday through Friday job, when my boyfriend doesn't. I'm not saying he doesn't work—he does. I can easily admit I thought he went to the facility, played some football, and then went home for the day. Nope, it couldn't be farther from the truth. He has early morning wake-up calls, on-the-field practice, workouts, game film, more practice, and then physical therapy on his aching muscles and bones. I think he works more during his season than I do in a year. Plus, people aren't trying to hit me all the time.

After forwarding the information to the legal department, I send an email to my new author, welcoming her to Willamette Publishing and letting her know how happy I am to work with her. I tell her what to expect in the next coming weeks and ask her to send a fresh copy of her manuscript to me so I can start working on it. I have the original printed off, but more often than not, the author has made changes and I want to make sure those are implemented.

I respond to a few more emails and then dig into the proposals I received overnight. This is normally the first thing I do every morning, but Basha threw me off with her thirst-trap videos of Alex. I'm not sorry she did, but her suggestion of sliding into his DMs without him knowing it's me isn't sitting right. I know people do this, and it makes me wonder if Alex has this issue.

And if he does, would he tell me about them?

An uneasy feeling takes over and while I try to shake it, I can't. I'm at a disadvantage here, with this whole social media video-making thing, and I don't like it.

## EIGHTEEN

## ALEX

It's game day.

During warm-ups, I scan the crowd for Kelsey. When I see her sitting with Autumn, a big smile takes over my face, going from ear to ear. It's not lost on me that I almost lost her. If I were her, I would've quit this relationship and never looked back. It doesn't matter how well you get along with someone or how fantastic the sex is —because believe me, I'm horny for her, twenty-four-seven —the shit the media pulled is unacceptable. I wanted to issue a statement but the PR team for the Pioneers thought doing so would cause more harm than good. Instead, I took jabs at them during on-field interviews. I'm not sure if my message has been received, but they have seemed to leave us alone for the most part.

Of course, there are still the fans out there, making videos of us. Those, I don't mind, as long as they're not bashing my honey.

*My honey.* What a freaking pet name this is. In all the years of dating Maggie, not once did I call her anything other than her name. But day two or three into being with

Kels and she's my honey. Sweet and tangy, not to mention sticky. Boy, I do love when she's stuck to me.

Kelsey finally waves, and like the fool in love that I am, I wave back. Trey Miller, our left tackle, bumps my shoulder and nods toward her.

"Does she have a friend? Sister?"

"She has two brothers if you want me to hook you up."

"Fuck off, Moore."

"Don't be a hater."

He shakes his head. "Be serious."

"She has two coworkers that I know of. One she hangs out with a lot, but I don't know much about her. Want to double date?"

He stares into the crowd and nods. "I think that would be nice."

I give him a sideways glance. "Ah, I didn't know you had a sweet bone in that hulk sized body of yours."

"You think I look like the Hulk?" He flexes but nothing happens since he's wearing pads. "I have been working out."

I roll my eyes. He weighs over three-hundred pounds, and his jersey barely covers his belly half the time. None of this fazes him though. He struts around like he's the next GQ model. It's all in the confidence you have, I suppose. I'm a big dude, but I like to keep things tight. I don't mind being someone's teddy bear, I just don't want to always look like one.

"You gonna hook me up?"

"Yep, I'll talk to Kelsey after the game. No promises though. We don't talk a whole lot about her coworkers."

"What do you talk about?" he waggles his eyebrows at me and makes a kissy face.

"How much of a perv you are," I say pointedly.

Trey's face goes blank, and I do everything I can to keep a straight face. "Bro. Not cool."

I slap him on the shoulder pad and then make my way toward the wall. I hadn't thought of asking Kelsey if she wanted to come on the field, so I didn't secure her a pass. That doesn't mean I can't go see her though.

Kelsey sees me walking toward her section and comes down the stairs. She leans over the rail and gives me a kiss. The crowd around us goes wild, and to say I'm shocked she does this is an understatement, but I happily kiss her back.

"I'm glad you're here."

"Me, too," she says, looking fucking adorable in my custom jersey, which is hands down one of the best purchases I've ever made. I try not to think about Maggie, and how she would wear my number on the clothes she had made, but never my jersey. I don't want to compare her and Kelsey but sometimes my mind goes there. I feel like I was meant to meet Kelsey, and we were meant to start down this path together.

"Will you wait for me after the game?"

She nods and bites her lower lip, killing me slowly. "I'll see you in the hallway afterward. Autumn said she'll take me."

"See you then, honey."

I head back to my team and let the lot of them give me shit for kissing my girl before the game. Those of us who have significant others don't really care what they think because someday it's going to be them. Hell, a few of the guys have girls back in their hometown, but they're all smart enough not to move until they have a ring on their finger. Well, I say they're smart, but that might be because I have a sister and wouldn't want her putting her life on hold for a man regardless of what he does for work.

After the coin toss, the defense takes the field. I sit down next to Noah, and when no one's around I spill my guts. "I think I'm in love."

"With the game. I hope," he says without taking his eyes off the playbook.

"You get me, Westbury." I cover my heart with my hand. He looks up and then around us.

"Is Kelsey here?"

"Yeah, with Autumn."

"That's good. Peyton likes her."

"You mean as long as we win, and I don't fuck up."

Noah closes the book and sets it on the bench next to him. "That game, it's not your fault," he says even though I don't believe him. It was my fault. I have one job and that's to get the ball into his hands. If I can't do that, what good am I to him or the team?

"Shit happens," he adds. "We've all had shitty games. If you remember correctly, when Peyton was in the hospital, I was a colossal fuck up. I thought for sure Walters was going to kick me off the team for insubordination, and if he had, I would've deserved it. I would do anything for Peyton. Absolutely anything."

"What if she goes to another team?"

Noah sighs. "This isn't the time or place for that discussion," he says as he looks around. "Come over tonight."

"I'll talk to Kels and see what she says. I don't want to make plans without her."

Noah laughs. "You're a good man, Alex."

"I'm trying."

THE FINAL HORN sounds and fireworks go off. We all gather around Noah and congratulate him as well as Julius and Chase, who made some spectacular diving catches. Of course, the opposing coach tossed his flag, and his objections were overturned. Sucks for him he could only do it twice. There's no doubt in my mind he would've kept throwing his red beanbag in the air every time we scored or had a first down. He was not a happy camper on the sidelines today. I'm going to thoroughly enjoy seeing him on ESPN later during the highlight reels.

The on-the-field reporter stops me for the first time in a month. I haven't felt like talking to the press, mostly because of the horrible game I had in North Carolina and how they've treated Kelsey. She's the one who reminded me it wasn't Fox Sports, ESPN, or any of the other stations that posted about her, it was the local media who are trying to go viral over something they've sensationalized.

"Alex, do you have a minute?"

"Sure, Trinity." She works for Fox Sports.

"You're three wins away from clinching the division title. How does that make you feel?"

I look around and form the politically correct answer in my head. "There's a lot of games left to be played, Trinity. We have some strong opponents and we have to go out every week and play our best game."

"A few weeks back, you sat out. At halftime, Coach Walter said your status was unknown. What kept you out of that pivotal game?"

*Well, it wasn't exactly pivotal if we're three wins away from clinching the division title now is it, Trinity?*

"I had a strained muscle and I felt like I couldn't do my job to the fullest of my ability."

"Does the loss weigh heavily on you?"

"Every loss does. We want to go out and win every game and make our way back to the Super Bowl. I gotta run."

I move off into the crowd and avoid any other reporters who come my way. The only other one I'm willing to talk to is Aiden Marchetti, the sports anchor from MCAX where Autumn works, but I don't see him and head toward the locker room. Because of the position I play, not too many people want to chat with me and I'm okay with it. They want the superstars like Noah, Cameron Simmons, and Brandon Garrison. I hiked the ball when Noah told me to, and I blocked some men to give him more time in the pocket—nothing extraordinary to report.

After I shower and dress, I find Kelsey in the hall with the other wives and girlfriends. I take her hand and lead her away from everyone without saying hi or giving her a kiss. We veer down another hall, and then another until we're far enough away from the people lingering. I drop my bag and back her up against the wall, my lips instantly on hers and my hand cupping her ass.

Her fingers push into my wet hair as she opens her mouth for me. Our tongues touch and we moan at the same time. I pick her up and her legs wrap around my waist, leaving her perfectly lined up to where I want to be, all the time.

Kelsey flexes her hips, rubbing herself against me. "Honey," I say in between kissing her beautiful mouth.

"I've missed you."

"I'm right here." And I am. I haven't left her side except when she goes to work, or I go to the stadium. I time everything so I'm done when she's finished at the office, but she often has to work from home at night, which I don't mind. I either play on my phone or read a book. As long as I'm with her, I don't care.

Kelsey pulls away and looks into my eyes. "I know but watching you out there, with all that bending over you do . . ." She fans her face.

I can't help but laugh and bury my face in her neck. "Honey, you're killing me right now."

"Take me home, then. To your house."

I quickly realized she's a bit more vocal in the bedroom when we're at my place, which I'm sure has to do with her neighbors. I don't mind in the slightest because hearing her scream my name out in pleasure is one of the purest joys I've ever experienced.

"I will, but first, Noah asked if we want to go over to his and Peyton's tonight."

"For another party?"

"No, he just invited us over because I asked him about his future with the team. I sense there's something he wants to tell me. And before you ask, I don't know if his dad is there. He could be, but he might have gone back to Los Angeles or wherever he lives."

"That's okay. I'm over him."

My eyebrow pops at her. "Is that so?"

She shrugs but looks away and starts laughing. "Okay, maybe not. I will be after I meet him, whenever that might be."

"You're incorrigible." I pepper her face with kisses until she squeals.

"Okay, let's go to Noah and Peyton's. It's not like what we have planned for later has a timer."

"This is true," I say after kissing her again. We go for another make-out session and then finally disengage when we hear people milling around. With her hand in mine, we zig-zag toward the exit and into the parking lot where I get the dubious honor of lifting her into my truck. Her ass fits perfectly in the palm of my hand, and I vow to never ever sell this thing as long as Kelsey and I are together.

## NINETEEN

KELSEY

As much as I want to make friends with Alex's friends and teammates, there are also times when I want to go home and be with him, alone. The more time we spend together, the more I want to be with him. It's a weird feeling, knowing my heart craves someone as much as it does with Alex, but I'm relishing the feeling. I think—no, I believe—he feels the same way. On the rare night we're not together and waking up in each other's arms the next day, he lets me know I'm the first thing on his mind with either a text or a phone call.

Alex stands behind me as the elevator to Noah and Peyton's climbs. The view of the city as dusk turns into night is spectacular. After living in New York City for so long, I thought I wouldn't be able to love another city, but I do. I'm certain it's because I've met Alex. If I hadn't, I'd be home right now with my red pen, marking up a manuscript. He's shown me so much of what the City of Roses has to offer, and I'm so grateful for him.

Our ride comes to a stop, and he kisses my neck. "We won't stay long," he whispers against my skin. To me, it's already long enough. I want to go home and spend the rest of the night in his arms before my workday begins tomorrow and we're thrown back into the same routine. Alex tells me that come February, life changes. He'll have time off to do whatever, except I won't. I don't have the luxury of taking weeks, or even months, off. I don't know if it's foolish to think that far ahead, months from now, and expect us to be together, but I'm hoping.

The elevator door opens. Alex tugs on my hand, but I hesitate. It's weird walking into someone's home without them welcoming you. As if Noah senses my hesitation, he comes around the corner with a grin on his face.

"Perfect timing," he says as a way to greet us. "My dad just put the meat on the grill. Dinner should be ready in a few minutes. Let's grab a drink."

*His dad!*

Nothing fazes Alex, and I wish I could be like him. He's used to this, the glitz and glam of entertainment. I spent more time than I care to admit looking him up on the internet again and saw just how many events he goes to. One thing I learned is he looks damn fine in a tuxedo. I also figured out he's camera shy and prefers to keep his head down. He doesn't like the limelight or the attention. Can't say I blame him.

My feet stumble and Alex looks at me. He shakes his head with a smirk and then we're walking again. This time out to the balcony where Liam Page is. Not only is he out here, but so is Harrison James.

*The dads!*

Alex clears his throat, and the men look in his direction. Every fiber of my being ignites with nervousness. "Gentlemen, I'd like to introduce you to my girlfriend,

Kelsey Sloane." Alex smiles at me and then says, "Kels, this is Liam and Harrison, Noah and Peyton's dads."

Their dads. Not members of a famous band or two extremely hot musicians. Tonight, they're fathers who are in town to visit their kids.

Liam is the first to shake my hand, and then Harrison. I'm tongue-tied and the words I think I should say don't make it from my brain to my mouth.

"Hi," I pause and clear my throat, along with giving myself a mental pep talk. I can do this. For God's sake, they're normal people. "Hi," I say with a bit more umph. "It's nice to finally meet you."

"You too," Harrison says. "Peyton told me you're new to town?"

"Yes, I moved here from New York for work."

"What do you do?" Liam asks.

"I work for Willamette Publishing as an acquisitions editor. I acquire manuscripts for publication."

"No shit?" Harrison says. "I've thought about writing my autobiography. I have a story to tell."

Liam bends over and lets out a roaring laugh. "You! Write a book?" he continues, with everyone watching. When he finally composes himself, he wipes at his pretend tears and straightens. "Okay. Yeah, you should do it."

"What in the hell was that?" Harrison asks.

Liam shrugs. "I had to pretend to be JD since he's not here."

"You're such an ass," Harrison says with a big grin on his face.

I watch the back and forth between them and wonder just how long they've been friends. The question is out of my mouth before I can stop it.

"I met Harrison shortly after I moved to Los Angeles. I was eighteen, almost nineteen." Liam tells me.

"And you've played together ever since?"

Harrison nods. "I used to be the house drummer at a music bar. This guy comes in one night to sing and the rest is history."

"And your kids meet and fall in love? That's just so . . . romantic."

"Yeah," Liam adds. The air between us shifts. It becomes thick with tension as Liam looks from me to Harrison, and then to the grill. "Not exactly how it's probably playing out in your head, but we'll run with your version. Makes things less messy." Liam takes the meat off the grill, turns off the gas, and walks into the penthouse.

"I said something wrong," I mumble these words to myself, but Harrison hears me.

"Don't be hard on yourself. There's a lot of history there, something Peyton or Noah can fill you in on another time." Harrison follows Liam, leaving Alex and me alone, and I'm feeling like a colossal idiot.

"Shit."

"Hey, it's okay," Alex says squeezing me against him in what I assume he intends to be a reassuring hug.

"No, it's not. Whatever I said, it was the wrong thing and now I've messed everything up."

"Hey, are you guys coming in?" Noah asks from behind us. I glance at Alex, pleading with him. I don't know what I did, but the idea of sitting down with them for dinner isn't something I want to do right now.

"I'm not feeling that great," Alex says to Noah. "I think we're going to head home."

"Really?"

He nods and never takes his eyes off mine. "Yeah. Raincheck?"

"Yeah, sure, of course."

Alex tells Noah that we'll see ourselves out and by the time we're in the elevator, tears stream down my face. "I fucked up."

"No, you didn't. I should've told you the entire story of their family. I'll start at the beginning." Alex fills me in on our way back to the parking garage, telling me about Liam's decision to drop out of college to start a career, unbeknownst to him that his ex-girlfriend was pregnant until he returned home ten years later to attend a funeral and came face to face with his son. By then, Liam had a successful music career and was all set to put it on hold so he could get to know his Noah when Harrison came to town and fell in love with Peyton's mom.

"Wow."

"It's a pretty heavy story."

"I didn't think Noah and Peyton had such a big age gap."

"They don't, I don't believe."

"Well, it's at least ten years if what you're telling me is true."

"Oh, no. I'm not done. The reason Liam returned to town is because Peyton's dad passed away. He and Liam were best friends growing up and he came back for the funeral. Harrison adopted Peyton and her sister Elle when they were seven or eight. If I remember correctly, Peyton and Noah are five years apart. They've been close their entire lives, but it wasn't until Peyton was in a car accident that things changed for them. I should've told you. It's not a secret, but Noah also doesn't go around telling people either. Most of his close friends know."

Alex helps me into his truck and after he gets behind the wheel, he pulls me closer. I rest my head on that comfort spot right below his collarbone. "I like this," he says.

"Mhm, me too." I stay like this until we get to my place. I perk up when my building comes into view. "I thought we were going back to your place. Are you staying here tonight?" I ask him after he parks. He nods, gets out of the truck and rushes to my side to help me out. With my feet on the ground, Alex kisses me, for all to see.

"I have a confession," he whispers into my ear.

"What's that?" I can't help but giggle from the sensation from his scruff.

"I like spending the night at your place."

"Why's that?" I can't imagine how my tiny apartment is comfortable for him at all. He's the gentle giant inside of there and can't spread out.

"Well, for one, I like your bed. It's small, which means you have no choice but to sleep in my arms." He's right, it is small compared to his king sized one.

"That's it?"

He shakes his head. "Another reason is because I like to hear your bed squeak when I thrust into you."

"Is that so?"

Alex nods. "That sound is so taboo, it excites me. But there's more."

"Okay."

"I like that you grip the railing of your headboard when you're riding me."

"And why's that?" I shift my weight from one foot to the other, to create some friction between my legs.

"Because"—he steps closer, backing me into the still open passenger side door and blocking me from view as he cups my breasts—"when you're using that rail, these beautiful fucking tits of yours slap me in the face. Between you bouncing on my dick and hitting me with your tits, it's the best damn thing ever."

"Alex," I say his name as if I'm out of breath. "We should go upstairs."

He nods. "We definitely should." Before he steps away, he takes my hand and places it over his crotch.

"I thought you didn't feel well." I joke.

"I don't," he says as he moves my hand up and down. "I think I need a nurse."

"Oh, God," I say quietly, unsure if he's heard me over the traffic. "Alex, we need to go inside before someone catches us out there."

He rests his head on my shoulder and nods. "I need a minute."

"Okay. Will it help if I put images in your mind."

"Depends on what kind of images you're talking about. If they are of any part of you, no they definitely won't help because I have such a fucking hard-on for you. All the time."

"Do you think about me at practice?"

"Sometimes, and now that you bring it up, I think about us fucking in the locker room, weight room, trainer's room. Hell, any place I frequent."

"Jesus."

"You're telling me, Kels. Right now, I can picture us fornicating all over the place. You, me, and our naked bodies."

I giggle. Alex freezes. "You said fornicate."

"Sorry, my bad, dirty girl. Fucking. I can picture us fucking all over the facility."

"You'd get fired."

"It'd be worth it."

"That's the wrong brain thinking. Anyway, granny panties."

"Are you wearing them?" He slips his hand down the back of my pants. "Nope," he says after giving my thong a tug. "Try again."

"Dentures."

He shakes his head. "Blow job without fear of being bit."

I look to the side, for any inspiration but see nothing except a woman standing not far from us with her phone pointed in our direction. I tell Alex and that seems to do the trick. He takes my hand and pulls me from the truck, shuts the door, and sets his alarm.

We rush across the street and duck into my building, saying nothing until we're at my front door. "It's hard being spontaneous when everyone is the paparazzi these days."

"I get it." Ever since the first couple of incidents with the media, they've left us alone. I'm grateful because I don't like feeling like I can't be myself. Plus, I like meeting up with my coworkers and they don't need their privacy invaded because of who I'm dating.

"Hey, you know what?" Alex says as we walk into the living room.

"What's that?"

He walks to me and pulls me into his arms. "I'm falling in love with you."

I search his eyes while my heart does a somersault and beats so fast, I fear he can hear it. I've long since fallen for him but hadn't told him, mostly out of fear he wasn't on the same page as me.

"Well, let me know when you're over the edge because I'll be waiting for you."

## TWENTY

ALEX

The Pioneers head into the Thanksgiving break with a sizable lead over our division rivals, making these few days relaxing. Of course, this puts a target on our back. We're the defending Super Bowl champions and like with any team, we want to be in the big game at the end of the year. We want to repeat as champions, and I know we can do it. We have the team that can get the job done. Especially when I'm doing my job and getting the ball into my QB's hands.

Kelsey lies next to me, with her head on my chest. Last night, she fell asleep while her fingers trailed the lines of my tattoo. I don't know what time I finally closed my eyes, but as I held her, I came to the realization that I want her here, in my space permanently. But then, I started thinking about how she'd get back and forth to work. I'm at least thirty minutes from downtown, and that's without traffic. Not to mention, she doesn't drive. Kelsey could easily take Rizzo, or I could pay for a car service.

Or I could sell my house and buy an apartment downtown. Except I don't want to live there. I love living up on the hill, away from the congestion and noise of the city. My backyard is an oasis, and it's private. I know I could have some privacy and more security in an apartment—not that I need that—but city life isn't for me. This place is, and I love where I live.

Kelsey stirs and I roll us onto our sides. Her hand trails up my chest, over my neck across my cheek and then her fingers trace my lower lip. I gently bite her finger, and in response, she hitches her legs over my hip.

"Hmm, good morning," she says as encounters my morning wood. I flex my hips and rub my dick along her folds. Kelsey moans and reaches between us to stroke my cock.

"Kels . . ." Her name comes out as a warning, but it's anything but. I'm a walking hard-on around her.

Her leg moves higher as she aligns herself for better access. My eyes roll back when the tip of my dick touches her sex. "You're wet, honey. Did you have a dirty dream about me?" I ask as my fingers push into her.

"Yes," she gasps, leaving me to wonder if it's a yes about the dream or the fact that I'm fingering her. I could push for an answer, but the truth of the matter is, I don't care. I know she thinks about me as much as I think about her.

I pull away from her and try to reach the nightstand to get a condom. It's not easy and my muscles strain.

"No condom."

Every part of me freezes. Slowly, I turn to face her. Kelsey's staring at me. "Kelsey?"

She nods. "You know I'm on the pill and . . ." She closes her eyes for a second and then looks at me again. "I want to feel you. All of you."

There aren't many things in life that can leave me speechless, but this is one of them. I swallow hard and try to form a response in my head, but nothing comes to mind. Well except every dirty thought possible like the obvious of rolling her over and plunging into her. *Way to ruin a moment.*

"Honey, are you sure?"

Kelsey tugs me back to my side and we're right back where we started. She strokes my erection, giving it a few pumps before lining me up with her sex. For whatever reason, it's like my body forgot how to function, and I think she knows this. She flexes and the tip is in, and then she moves and I'm not.

*What the fuck?*

Again, with another arch. Her eyes roll back and then I'm out again.

I lose track of how many times she does this until I feel my balls tighten. I haven't even been fully sheathed in her and I'm about to come.

"Honey . . ." The word comes out strangled. "Fuck, Kels. I'm going to come."

She doesn't care though and keeps this up. Taking the tip of my cock into her and then pulling out. The back and forth, and the tiny gasps she lets out each time I enter her, are killing me.

Kelsey pushes me onto my back and then straddles my hips. Her hands push on my chest while slowly taking in every inch of me. I try to watch my dick disappear into her, but I swear I lose consciousness.

"Fuck me," I utter the words as she starts the rise and fall. My hand rests on her hips and I help guide her up and down until she moves my hands to her breasts.

"Squeeze." One single word has my hips thrusting into her. I do as she commands, tweaking her nipples and palming her glorious tits. I let go for a moment to watch them bounce. The sight spurs me to sit up and play catch a titty with my mouth. When I finally latch on to a nipple, I smile and suck. And then I start over with her other breast.

"Alex . . ."

I don't even need to ask what she wants or needs. I know my girl. Wrapping my arm around her waist, my hand grips her hip and helps her move faster, and my free hand finds her bud. It's fucking swollen and like a damn beacon between her folds. As soon as I had a little pressure, her head falls back, her hips rock faster and her nails dig into my shoulder blades.

"Alex . . . Alex . . ."

"Yeah, baby. I'm there."

When I feel her getting close, I flex into her and keep the pressure on her clit. "I'm there, honey."

"Yes . . . yes . . . oh, God . . . Alex . . ." She screams my name as her walls squeeze my cock. The sensation is too much to take, and I pump wildly into her, letting go. My hands move to her hips and hold her as she rides the aftershocks of her orgasm. She collapses against me, and I hold her a moment before sliding out of her and heading to the bathroom.

When I return, she's spread-eagle on my mattress staring at the ceiling.

"Are you alive?"

"Barely." She accepts the tissues from me but gets up and heads to the bathroom. I'm sitting on the edge of the bed when she saunters back into the room, wearing one of my T-shirts. She comes to me and straddles my lap.

"I'm not complaining, but where did that come from?"

Kelsey shrugs. "I think the book I'm editing. I don't know, she had this scene and I kept picturing it in my mind, and then I had a dream, and there you were, ready to go."

"I'm always ready for you." I kiss her and smile when I taste her minty tongue. "Brushed your teeth, huh?"

She laughs and nods. "I couldn't resist."

"Can we talk about the lack of protection?" I ask, needing to make sure she's good with the decision. "Again, not complaining, but I am surprised."

"Sorry," she says as she runs her fingers through my hair. "I meant to bring it up before, but it's awkward."

"It is, but definitely something we should talk about. I want you to be one hundred percent sure about this decision."

"I am," she says as she bites lower lip. "And it felt really good."

"Fuck yeah, it did." I pull her to me and roll us onto the bed. She spreads her legs and I settle between them. "Now I don't have to worry about having a condom with me all the time."

"Nope, you don't."

"And we can be really spontaneous."

"Yes, we can."

The doorbell chimes and we both look in the direction of the front door. "Did you order food?" Kelsey asks.

"Nope, and I'm not expecting anyone." I wait a minute, hoping whoever is at the door will go away, but the bell sounds again.

It pains me to leave Kelsey. She laughs when I put on my gray sweats.

"You better come back to me."

"Give me a minute to get rid of whoever is at the door and then I'll come back, I want to read this book with you," I tell her. "I want to see what else we can try today, since neither of us have work." I kneel on the bed and kiss her, which turns into a small groping session until the bell chimes again for the third time. I groan and head to the living room. "I'm coming. Jesus!" Only it's the wrong kind of coming I want to do right now. Knowing Kelsey is in the other room gives me every incentive to get rid of whoever is at my house.

I open the door, prepared to tell them to get lost when I come face-to-face with Maggie.

A very pregnant Maggie.

With luggage.

*What the actual fuck?*

"Surprise!" she says as she steps into the house and pulls me into a hug. "You're surprised right? I know I should've called or sent a text, but I wanted to see your face." She grabs my cheeks and gives them a squeeze. "I've missed you so much."

"Definitely a surprise." I make no attempt at hugging her back and for whatever reason my eyes don't leave her suitcases.

"Can you bring those in for me?" Maggie eyes her belly and then me.

*What in the actual fuck!*

Without thinking, I go out and grab the overly heavy bags and bring them inside. "When did you get back?"

"About two hours ago."

"And you came right here?" I ask, slamming the door. She doesn't seem fazed and walks into the living room to sit down.

"Where else would I go?"

Certainly not the home we sold when she decided to move to London. Maybe a former coworker? One of her friends, perhaps? Definitely not her ex's! I run my hand over my hair and look down the hall where Kelsey's waiting for me. Maggie's on my couch, making herself comfortable. I look at her, sitting there, with her round belly and every ounce of life I have drains from me. If she's here, it's because that baby she's carrying is mine. And that means she kept this pregnancy from me, which is unacceptable.

Fear takes over. I'm going to lose Kelsey over this—something I knew nothing about. With heavy steps, I make my way back to my bedroom thinking about what to say to Kelsey and run every scenario through my mind. In an ideal, fake world, Kelsey goes out to the living room and embraces whatever the fuck is happening out there. But life isn't like that. She's going to be hurt.

Kelsey's sitting up in bed, with a book in her hands. She smiles when she sees me and then it drops, probably when she sees the grim expression on my face. "What's wrong?"

"Maggie's here."

"Oh." her eyes dart to the door and then back at me. "Were you expecting her?"

I shake my head slowly. "I think she needs a place to stay. She brought her luggage and then some."

"What are you talking about?"

I begin to pace. "Fuck!"

"Alex, what's going on?" Kelsey comes to me and pulls my hands out of my hair. "She told me she was coming back but I didn't ask when because it doesn't matter, but she's here and fuck . . ."

"I'm confused, are you saying she plans to stay here?"

I nod and my stomach rolls. I'm going to be sick.

"Well, she can go to a hotel or something."

"There's more."

"What?"

"She's pregnant."

Kelsey steps back and looks at me before she looks at the bed—the bed where we just had the most amazing sex—and then back at me. "Clearly, it's not yours so what's the big deal?"

Everything in me dies. I don't make a habit of discussing my sex life with anyone, including people I'm dating, but this might be one of those times when being as honest as possible might come in handy.

"About six or seven months ago, Maggie came back for a visit. We hooked up while she was here."

"Oh," Kelsey says quietly. "Is it yours? Co-could it be yours?"

I nod but then shrug. I don't know shit about pregnancy. "I don't know. I didn't ask."

Kelsey stares at me for a long moment and then starts moving around the bedroom. Before I can comprehend everything, she's dressed, and her bag is packed. "What are you doing?"

"I have to go."

"Where? We have plans."

"I just . . ." She shakes her head and tries to go past me. I pull her to me and cup her cheek. "I don't know what's going on in that head of yours, but please stop. I didn't know she was coming or why she's here. I haven't spoken to her since her friends pulled that shit with the gala."

"You spoke to her about that?"

*Shit.* "Not exactly. She texted me and I told her to tell them to knock it off."

"Why didn't you tell me?"

"I didn't think it mattered. I can show you the text messages. I don't make speaking to my exes a habit. They're an ex for a reason."

"But you said yourself that the breakup was hard on you."

"Are you seriously throwing something I said months

ago, on our first date, in my face right now?" I step back from her and shake my head. "Look, I don't know what's going on, but I don't like it."

"Well, I don't like it either."

"I'm talking about you too, Kelsey. You're acting like I've done something wrong." I point toward the wall. "I didn't invite her, and I certainly didn't know she was pregnant."

"Because if you did, you'd be with her?"

I don't answer her. I don't know how to.

Kelsey pulls her phone out. "My Uber will be here in five. I'll go wait outside."

"Stop!" I say as I try to reach for her, but she steps out of my way. "Kelsey, this is ridiculous. I didn't know."

"I get it, Alex. I do. But it sounds like you need to figure some shit out. I'm going to go out the door here, I don't want to meet her."

I don't even know what to say and let her leave through the slider in my bedroom. She doesn't slam the door or run through the yard. I watch her until I can't see her anymore. I don't know how long I stand there until I move. After I change, I head back into the living room and find Maggie lying on the couch with the television on.

"Is it mine, Maggie?"

She mutes the TV and sits up. "I don't know, Alex."

## TWENTY-ONE

## KELSEY

I lose track of how many minutes or hours pass since I left Alex's in haste. I had to get out of there, knowing Maggie—a very pregnant Maggie according to Alex— was sitting in the living room. It doesn't take anyone with any common sense to figure out what Alex was doing in his room, and I swear she saw me ducking tail through the backyard.

But she didn't come out and stop me.

My intercom rings and I know it's Alex before I even answer it. He came for me, which I didn't expect him to do, but hoped he would. Still, I think I need some space from him and . . . well everything. Being with him should be easy, but our relationship seems everything but.

Everywhere I turn, Maggie is there. The other wives and girlfriends talk about her in front of me at the games. The media loves her, even though she's not here, and broke his heart. Everyone misses her. Now she's back . . . at his house . . . and she's pregnant.

I go to the wall and press the button, trying to sound as normal as possible but my voice breaks. "Hello?"

"Hey, Kels. It's me."

Those words break me. I don't care how many times I've heard them, they affect me the same way each and every time, only now they hurt because I don't know if I'll ever hear them again after this moment.

"Kelsey," he says my name again and I shake my head even though he can't see me. "Honey, I need to see you. Please."

I look to the left and see the auto generated code blinking. I repeat the numbers to him, although fairly inaudibly and then release the intercom button. He either heard me or he didn't. I'm not sure I'm in the right mind to care.

After a minute, I open the door and walk the few feet down the hall to meet the elevator. I pull my sweater tightly around me when the number pauses on my floor. The doors open and Alex steps out. He's not the usual Alex I'm used to seeing. He's wearing jeans and a hoodie, and his eyes are red rimmed. It pains me to keep my hands to myself and not reach for him, to collapse in his arms, but he's not mine, and I'm not sure he ever has been.

Alex steps toward me, but I step back and shake my head. He sighs. "I'm sorry, Kels."

He could mean he's sorry for a million different things, but my mind only goes to one. "The baby's yours, isn't it?"

He hesitates and I know.

"She's not sure."

God, that's awful for both of them.

"Can we go to your place and talk?" he asks.

I eye my door. It's ideal, but I know that once I'm in that tiny place, and he's there . . . "I don't think that's a good idea."

"Right," his voice cracks and then he clears his throat.

"I'll keep this quick then. I love you, Kels. I thought I needed to wait until the right time to say the words, but something tells me my time has expired, and I wanted you to know. I knew I'd fall hard for you from the moment I saw you standing there with Myles. From then to our first dinner and then our date, you made sense to me. I had to figure out a way to see you again, so I came up with the idea for the football book because that meant we'd work side by side, and just being next to you was worth it for me. I didn't even fight the fall because everything screamed you were the one for me.

"And today . . ." he pauses and looks down at his feet, wiping the wetness away from his cheeks. "I didn't know, honey. I had no idea she was going to show up and I definitely didn't know she was pregnant. I would never put you in a position like that. I can't even imagine what's going through your mind, but I wish you'd tell me so we can work through this. I don't deserve this from you, Kels."

He's right, he doesn't.

"I know and I'm sorry. It's just . . ." My hands go to my hair and then back across my midsection. It's as if I'm hiding the gaping wound in my chest from him. "I don't know if I can do this, Alex."

"What do you mean?"

"I mean us. There's just so much that comes with being your girlfriend. Maggie, a maybe pregnancy, the media, her friends. It's never-ending."

"And if the baby isn't mine?"

"Is there even a chance of that?" I look in his eyes for the answer and see it and the realization guts me. Maggie thinks the baby is his. I feel bad for him and desperately want to hug him but I'm afraid it'll send the wrong message.

"I love you, Kels. Please don't do this." His voice breaks

and he reaches for me. "Please." I let him start to pull me to him but stop and drop my head until it touches his chest, putting distance between us. His hand rests on my shoulder and then drops.

"I can't, Alex."

"Yeah, I hear ya." He sighs and moves, and I stand tall. He turns his back to me and presses the button for the elevator. The doors open and he steps in. If I expected some romantic grand gesture to happen like I read in books, where we make eye contact and everything shifts, I don't realize it until the doors are closed. I'm barefoot, and now must rush down the stairs to catch him before he leaves in a taxi, but it doesn't happen.

Instead, Alex leans against the side wall so I can't see him, and I don't move until the doors are closed.

## HE DOESN'T GIVE UP.

I'm not sure if I expected him to or not, but every time I see his name on my phone or hear his voice, I break down. I thought my tears would've long dried up by now, but they keep coming. He calls and texts every day to let me know that he loves me. I know someday soon, he'll stop, and I'll break down all over again because that'll mean he's moved on.

Today, I'm meeting with my client, Fern—the one writing the football book. Thankfully, her character is the quarterback—a wild playboy type who gets tamed by the sweet innocent fan who he happens to meet at a party. It has the happily ever after that people look for, but I still hate it. In fact, I've ignored every pitch I received this week. None of them jump out of me and honestly, I'm over romance. Especially anything that has to do with the secret baby trope. There is absolutely no excuse for what Maggie has done to Alex in keeping her pregnancy a secret.

A young woman waves as I approach the table. She has yet to send in her headshot for the cover of her book so I'm happy she knows what I look like.

"Hi, Ms. Sloane. I'm so happy to meet you in person." Fern stands and holds her hand out to shake mine.

"Hi, Fern. Please, call me Kelsey. How was your trip?" I set my bag down and drape my jacket over the back of my chair.

"It's a super easy drive from Eugene."

"You know, I had no idea you were so close when we started all of this. I'm glad we could meet."

"Me too."

The waitress comes and takes our drink order and leaves us to look over our menus. Once we've both decided what we're going to get, we close them.

"What's Eugene like?" I ask her.

"It's nice," she says. "Like with every city, it has its good and bad. I'm a huge Ducks fan so it's nice being there."

"Oh, I like ducks."

Fern laughs. "No, the Oregon Ducks. It's a college in Eugene. They have a good football team."

My mouth makes an oh. I didn't know football when she submitted her story, and I don't know it now. Despite Alex trying to teach me.

The waitress returns with our drinks, and we place our order for food. "Do you have plans after lunch?"

"No," she says. "I'll probably hit the malls because

they're much bigger than what we have down there, but other than that, nothing."

"The offices aren't far from here. I could give you a tour. Although I warn you, they're small. We are hoping to grow in the next year or so, adding more editors."

"I'd love it and I don't mind small. It's the reason I chose Willamette Publishing. I figured I'd get more attention if I'm not competing with hundreds of other authors."

"Very valid point."

During lunch, we make idle chit-chat about anything we can think of. She tells me how fictionalized her story is, and that in real life, her high school boyfriend went away to college, with promises of returning, and never did. She's not eagerly waiting for any second chance anything because he's now married with five kids, and while he's still very hot, he passed the DILF stage after the second child.

"What's he now?" I ask, thinking back to the conversation Alex and I had on the whole DILF subject.

"He's someone who would have to pay a shit ton of child support if he left his wife."

"Oh, another valid point."

"Like I said, that ship sailed a long time ago. He never even came back to town. His parents divorced and both moved away. Any chance we had went out the door a long time ago."

"Did he at least tell you?"

Fern shakes her head. "Nope. The ultimate ghosting."

"Harsh," I say. "Well, if you can twist this into something, send it to me. I'd like to take a look and make an offer. I really liked what you did with the football story and have enjoyed working with you."

"Really?" She covers her heart with her hand. "Oh, wow. Thank you, Kelsey."

Once I've paid the tab, we walk back toward the office. I'm not really paying attention to my surroundings until I look up. Everything around me becomes a blur except for the two figures across the street—Alex and Maggie. They're standing next to a building I know has doctor's offices in it. He's dressed in slacks and wearing a long pea coat, not the way he used to dress when he was with me, or maybe this is normal for him. Maggie brushes something off his jacket and then kisses him. He doesn't push her away or turn his cheek to her.

I've seen enough and don't care to ever see him again. I pull my phone out of my pocket and send him a text.

> Don't contact me again.

For whatever reason, I stand there, waiting to see if he even acknowledges his phone. His hand goes into his pocket, and he looks at the screen, and then he's frantically looking around.

> ALEX MOORE
>
> Where are you?
>
> If you saw her kiss me, it's not what it looks like.
>
> Please, Kelsey

I stare at the messages on my phone and ignore them, stuffing my hands in my pocket and meeting Fern's gaze.

"Everything okay, Kelsey?"

"Yeah, everything's fine."

Except nothing's fine. He got over me as fast as I got under him. That's my fault. I knew better than to sleep with him. To think I told him no condom; the thought makes me both sad and angry. I've read enough novels to know athletes are playboys, each and every one of them. Alex is no different, in fact he lives up to the stereotypical trope because he got his heart broken. Mr. I-Can't-Give-You-My-Heart-Cos-It's-Broken. The moment Maggie came back, I knew things were over between us. She fits into his world, where I'm just an outsider, watching his fast-paced life rush by in a blur.

As Fern and I make our way to the office, I pull my phone out and leave myself a note to buy a pregnancy test. I'm not late and I'm on the pill, but with my luck, his sperm are superhuman and can break through every scientific barrier out there.

By the time Fern yells, "Watch out," my head smacks against the concrete wall surrounding the park and I land on my arm. I don't know if it's the pain in my head that hurts more than the one in my arm. Either way, I need help.

## TWENTY-TWO

ALEX

I've never been a man down on his luck until now, and I could easily blame Maggie, but when it comes down to it, it's on me. There's a long list of things I should've done differently. Not only with Maggie, but definitely with Kelsey. She's my priority and I should have put her feelings first, especially after the fiasco with the photos from the gala. I didn't do that.

When Maggie told me she was returning to Portland I should've made it clear that I'd moved on. I didn't and now I'm in this pickle.

In more ways than one.

Watching Kelsey leave out my bedroom slider and run across my yard put me at my lowest. Worse than the bullshit with the photos. I'm thankful I don't have a game this week otherwise I'd be a waste of space on the field. This shit should've never happened, and I should have never allowed Maggie in my house without checking with Kelsey first. She is the only one who matters.

Except for the baby Maggie's carrying.

My world spins on a tilted axis right now. I don't know

how to stop it or change it. Everything seems to be out of my control, and I don't get how I messed up so badly. It's not as if I cheated on Kelsey, but I guess I wasn't exactly upfront with her, either. Yet, here I am, dressed in a suit to go to a doctor's appointment for a baby that may or may not be mine.

Talk about another low blow.

There isn't a doubt in my mind, my question about paternity hurt Maggie's feelings but seeing her there at my front door hit me hard. Why not tell me? Why keep it? Believe me, this isn't a good surprise. It's a hurtful one. Not only to me, but to Kelsey as well, and she doesn't deserve to be hurt.

Outside, after the appointment that I didn't need or want to be at, Maggie acts like we're together. She brushes lint off my jacket—the one I don't want to wear—and kisses me, despite me making my feelings toward her very clear.

"Stop." I dodge her hand from touching my face.

"Why?"

"Because you know why," I tell her as my phone chimes. "We're not together."

"We could be. What if the baby's yours?"

*What if?*

I don't have an answer for her. The noble thing is to be with her, but I don't love her. I'm in love with Kelsey, and in the few days Maggie's been back, I've realized Maggie's not the one for me. I don't like who I am when I'm with her.

"Alex, we didn't even need to break up when I moved."

"Yet, we did. Proving that nothing good comes from a hook-up because now you're pregnant, and according to that chart you showed me, your conception date is either the day you left or the day after, which means as soon as you got to London you fucked someone. Where's he at? Why isn't he here going to your appointments?"

"Don't be crass," she says as she huffs and ignores my questions. Still, I want to know where the other guy is. And I can't help but wonder if they were a couple when she came back to visit? When did they start dating?

I pull my phone out and my face lights up when I see Kelsey's name but falls instantly when I see what she sent. I look around, sensing she's near and quickly type back, asking where she is.

"Fuck."

"What's wrong?"

"Well, if I had to take an educated guess, Kelsey saw us together."

Maggie looks around, as if it's going to make a difference. "Well . . ." She shrugs and looks at her phone.

"What do you mean, well? I'm in love with her, Maggie, and you put me in this situation."

"And what do you want me to do about that, Alex?"

"Gee, I don't know. Not fuck someone within hours of leaving me. Or how about getting a damn DNA test so I'm not stuck in fucking limbo, wondering if I'm losing the best person to ever come into my life."

"Do you seriously mean that?"

I give her my best pointed look. "Yes, I do."

"Are you saying you regret our relationship?"

"No, I'm not," I sigh. "But we ended, and I met the person I'm meant to be with, and now she wants nothing to do with me. Being in a relationship with an athlete is hard enough, but being in one with me, when you're looming over her all the time is daunting. Shit shouldn't be this hard."

I start walking up the street, away from Maggie even

though it pains me to leave her there in her condition. I need a moment away from her. My life cannot be about her, not anymore. I tug at the tie around my neck and stick it into my pocket and undo the top two buttons of my shirt. When I turn around, Maggie's walking toward me, focusing on her phone.

"You're going to walk into something if you don't pay attention to where you're going."

"I can multitask."

"Of course, you can."

This is the last place I want to have this conversation, but she's forced my hand. "Look, I asked for a test the other day, and I want it done. Your doctor said you can do it, so schedule it. It's not right to make me wait. I have a right to know."

"Can't you just wait until the baby's here?"

I shake my head. "No. I'm not going to sit in limbo while I'm trying to fix my relationship with Kelsey. She's far too important for me not to fight for her."

Maggie huffs. "Do you want me to talk to her?"

I scoff. "Fuck no. You've done enough."

"All I did was show up at your place."

"And invited yourself in like you own it, without zero consideration for me or for her. You should've called first, but no, you wanted the shock factor that came with knocking on my door to announce your return. I'm sorry, but none of this is okay."

"You're yelling and people are staring," she grits out.

"I don't care, Maggie," I say, pleading with her. "The woman I'm in love with wants nothing to do with me, because of you. Because of . . ." I can't bring myself to blame the baby she's carrying because no child should ever be blamed for how their parents fuck up. "Look, you know that if the baby is mine, I'll be there. But until then, I need you out of my house. You have a ton of friends who will let you stay with them until you find a place. I'm just not one of them. I can't be."

I walk away, leaving her on the street, knowing she won't follow. I need space from her, from the situation she's put me in. After walking in circles for over thirty minutes, I end up in front of Kelsey's office building.

"Fuck it," I say to myself as I go in. I'm prepared to turn the charm on when I get to the reception counter, but because I've been here before, they know me and issue me a pass right away. When I get to her floor, I approach Robin, Willamette Publishing's front desk receptionist, with a smile.

"Good afternoon, Robin. How are you today?"

"I'm good, Mr. Moore. I don't see you on Ms. Sloane's calendar today."

"No, I was in the neighborhood and wanted to chat about the edits on my book. Is she here?"

Robin looks over her shoulder and then shakes her head. "She didn't return from lunch."

*Fuck.*

"Is she working from home today? I can stop over there."

Another shake. "She's at the hospital."

My heart drops to the floor. "Wh-what?"

"Look, I'm not supposed to say anything—"

"I won't tell anyone," I interrupt her.

She nods. "Ms. Norris rushed out, saying Ms. Sloane had an accident and was in the emergency room."

"Do you know which hospital?" I ask as I shift from foot to foot. I know she's protecting Kelsey, but I need to get to her. Now. Not later. My fingers tap on the marble top of her desk. "Please," I beg.

"Legacy."

"Thank you, Robin." I forgo the elevator and rush down the stairs. As soon as I'm outside, I run toward Legacy, knowing I can beat a cab ride or arranging a rideshare on foot. Thankfully, when people see me running toward them, they part and give me as wide a birth as possible. The last thing I want to do is collide with someone because of my weight and speed; they'd go flying and that wouldn't be good for them.

When I arrive at the building, I'm out of breath, and think Coach would be proud of me, although he'd question my sanity. Inside, while still out of breath, I ask to see Kelsey Sloane.

"Are you her husband?"

"Yes," I say, lying.

"Alex?"

I turn at the sound of my name and find Basha standing there. I go to her. "What's going on?"

"How did you find her here?"

"It doesn't matter. What happened?"

Basha looks over my shoulder and then back at me. "She doesn't want you here," she says quietly.

I run my hand through my hair. "Basha, please. I love her."

"Look, I don't agree with either of you, but I know she loves you, too."

I can't help the smile that spreads across my face and I'm tempted to kiss Basha for just admitting what I already felt from Kelsey.

"Stop," she says, and I erase my smile. "I don't know what happened earlier, but she fell outside. She broke her arm and hit her head pretty bad. She has a concussion."

"Fuck. This isn't how things are supposed to be."

She nods. "No, they're not. Kelsey's good people, Alex. She's really hurt over all of this."

"And I'm not?" I shake my head and take a deep breath. "I'm sorry for snapping. I'm frustrated and angry."

"Yeah, I get it."

"I need to see her."

Basha waits a beat or two before nodding. "Come on, I'll take her to you. But you have to tell her you promised to hook me up with one of your teammates or something."

"Tell me which one and I'll do it."

"I'll send you the list." We stop at the front desk. "Hi, I'm going to take Ms. Sloane's husband back to see her. I'm Basha Norris, I'm the one who brought her in."

The woman behind the desk types and then nods toward us as she hands a sticker for me to put on my coat that reads, visitor. I follow Basha around a corner and down a hall. She points to a room with a closed door.

"She's in there. Good luck, Alex. I like you so I hope this works."

"Thanks, Basha. I like you too and I'm going to need all the luck you can muster."

"She's good people," Basha reiterates. "Like really good and she's afraid you're going to break her heart, worse than it's already breaking."

I frown and nod. "That's the last thing I want to do."

Basha leaves me standing at the door. I've never been so nervous in my life and pray Kelsey can't reach anything sharp to stab me with or throw at me. I knock and wait for her to say come in.

She's somewhat facing the wall, away from the door,

and doesn't look at me when I walk in. I stand a safe distance from her, just in case.

With a deep sigh, I say her name, "Kels."

She turns sharply and glares at me. "Get out. No wait, how did you find me? Never mind, I don't care."

"Please don't say you don't care about me." I can't bear knowing she hates me this much. I inhale deeply and work to keep my voice from cracking. "How I found you doesn't matter. What matters is I'm here, where I want to be."

"I don't want you here, Alex." She turns away again. I take a step closer to the bed and reach out for her, but pull my hand back before touching her. I can feel her slipping away from me, and it hurts. My heart breaks like nothing I've ever felt before. Kelsey is the one for me and I have to find a way to prove to her I'm the right man for her.

"I know and I accept that, but I need you to hear me and if what I have to say isn't enough, I'll go, and you'll never hear from me again. I don't know if you remember what I said the other day in the hall, but I love you. I'm in love with you, Kels. I know words don't make up for actions. I get that. I'm sorry that I hurt you by keeping secrets. That was never my intention. Believe me when I tell you this, I had no idea Maggie was pregnant. To make things worse, I don't even know if I'm the father or not because of her actions, and I feel like not knowing hurts us."

"I won't be the reason a child doesn't have both its parents."

"I can still be a dad without being with the baby's mother." I take a couple of steps toward Kelsey.

"You love Maggie," her voice breaks, which in turn crumbles every part of me.

"No, I *loved* her. But now that I know what real love feels like I know I was never in love with Maggie. Not in the way I love you, Kels. I don't even like the person I am when she's around. I'm angry all the time, I'm miserable. All I want to do is snuggle on your couch and watch TV or read a book with you. Having her at my house, it's exhausting. From the moment the sun comes up to when it goes down, she's demanding all of my time. It's all about being social for her and that's not who I am or want to be."

"So, you're back together?"

"What?" I'm confused by her question and then I realize what I said makes it seem like we're together. "Hell no, honey. She's at my house until she finds a place. Or she was. I told her she needs to be gone before I get home tonight. But while she was there, these past few days, she's taken over everything like we are back together, and it's made me realize how much I hate it."

I take another step closer and instead of trying to reach for her, I push my hands into my pockets. Her verbal rejection is enough to last me a lifetime. The last thing I need to see, or feel is her physically pushing me away.

"What I'm saying or trying to say is since meeting you, you've shown me what kind of life I want to have. That the routine we created together makes me so fucking happy and without you I'm miserable. I don't like me right now."

"I don't like you now, either."

"I know, honey." Two more steps closer. "I want to make you like me again. Maybe even love me."

She glances at me with tears coming down her face. I close the gap and gently wipe them away. "I don't want to ever make you cry, Kelsey."

She nods but is unable to say anything because the tech comes in to set her arm. Once the cast is on and he leaves the room, I help Kelsey put her coat on. "Can I take you home?"

"Look, Alex. I need some time. All of this, it's too much. Maggie . . . I saw her kiss you today, and if you're the father of her baby, I don't want to have anything to do with any of it. She clearly feels differently, and after all the crap with her friends and the media, it's never going to stop. I'm sorry, I just can't."

"Kels, please don't do this," I plead but she doesn't say anything. I step back and look down at the ground to hide my own tears. "I understand. Can I at least make sure you get home?"

"I'll be fine."

It pains me to leave her in the room by herself, but I do. When I get back to the waiting room, I tell Basha that she's ready, and then I leave. I don't know what else I'm supposed to do, except beg, but I'm not even sure that'll work.

## TWENTY-THREE

# KELSEY

The flight to Buffalo took forever, or at least it seemed to. I'm sure the fly time was normal, but when you don't want to go home, and yet it's the only way to get away from your life choices, everything drags on.

My dad, Mel, meets me at baggage claim and hugs me for a long time while I cry into his chest. I didn't fail even though that's what it feels like. I went out to Portland with the intention of advancing my career and being successful. I'm home because I need a break. I need to not see Alex everywhere I go or be at his disposal. I need time to heal and not see him on television or walking down the street. Everything about my time with him hurts. Even though I never said those three words that can easily change a relationship, he knew. And I told Basha. For me, it was love at first sight. The lust part came by the end of the night. Hook-ups aren't my thing, but I would've hooked up with him if we had met under different circumstances.

"It's okay, sweetie," my dad says as he rubs my back. "Mom has soup on the stove for you."

"I don't need soup," I tell him. My parents think soup fixes everything.

Dad steps back and keeps both his hands on my shoulders. "But you're hurt." He eyes my cast because he can see the physical pain, not the emotional stuff. Sometimes I wish people could see a broken heart because then maybe they'd think twice about their actions.

"My arm will be fine, Daddy. Come on, I gotta get my luggage."

When we walk over to the carousel and my brother, Dalton, is there, waiting for my suitcases. He pulls me into a side hug and kisses the top of my head. "Whose ass do I need to kick?"

I laugh. The image of Dalton and Alex going at it is funny. Dalton wouldn't stand a chance against my footballer.

No, I can't call him my anything. Not anymore.

"I appreciate it, but I'll be okay." Eventually.

Dalton and my dad take care of my bags, with me following behind. Thankfully, Dalton drove, which means we'll get to my parents in a reasonable amount of time. We're about an hour south, but my dad insists on driving under the speed limit, where Dalton will go at least ten over.

My brother holds the door open for me while I crawl into the back of his SUV. He tries to buckle me up, but I bat his hands away. "I'm not an invalid," I tell him.

"Does mom know this?"

I stick my tongue out at him.

When I told my mom about Alex, she suggested I come home for a visit, telling me I can recharge here and then face things with a fresh outlook. I didn't agree until I fell and fractured my arm and ended up with a minor concussion. Granted, the break is tiny, and I only have to wear my cast for three weeks. It was this or figure things out on my own. I could've managed, but there's something about having your mom take care of you. It wasn't until Dalton told me he booked a flight out that night that I packed my stuff and took a cab to the airport.

I close my eyes for the fifty-minute car ride. When the crunch of gravel sounds under the tires, I open them and find my mom, Tilly, standing on our front porch, wearing an apron. If she's anything, she's the poster for small-town living. If I had to guess, I bet she's made a half dozen pies for church on Sunday and there isn't a single hair out of place from the everyday bun she wears. People would be shocked if they ever saw her with her hair down, which goes well past her waist. I can't remember a single time she ever got her hair cut while I was growing up.

Dalton opens the door for me and tells me he'll get my bags. I make my way up the stairs and fall into my mom's embrace. The tears return this time, but with more force.

"Come on, baby girl, let's get you inside."

She holds me until we're in my bedroom, sitting on my bed. Not much has changed in here, except it's clean and dust free. My awards still sit on the floating shelves, and there's a framed copy of the *New York Times* bestsellers list from when the book I acquired made the list. It doesn't matter that my name isn't anywhere on there, my parents are proud.

Dalton and my dad bring my luggage in and then we hear the back door shut. They're heading to the barn to do "man's work" at least that's what my dad calls it. I know he likes to take advantage of Dalton being in town to get some of the heavier stuff done around here.

"I feel like such a failure."

"No, no," she says. "None of this is your fault."

"I know but I can't help but feel like I'm not enough to fit into his world. I really like him, Mom."

"Nonsense, he needs to fit into yours. Just because he's some fancy football player doesn't mean he walks on water."

"That's just it. He's so much more than the guy you see on TV. It's this life he led with his ex. It's fancy with its parties and gatherings. Mom, the dress he paid for was over a thousand dollars, and it was one of the cheapest ones the personal shopper showed me. Like, that's not me. I live off a budget and clip coupons. And now that his ex is back . . ." I trail off.

My mom shakes her head. "I will never understand why people don't use condoms."

I roll my eyes. "People do. They break." Thank God she will never know about what I said to Alex during our last time together. She'd find a way to ground me and make me repent to her pastor.

She leaves me to unpack. It's slow and frustrating because I can only use one hand, but I appreciate the quiet. After a while, Dalton comes in and finds me lying on my bed, staring at my ceiling.

"Wanna ride into town with me?" he asks.

I don't but sit up anyway and tell him I'll go. It's been a hot minute since I've been back to town for any extended period of time. Once I started college, I stayed on campus during the summer to work, and then I got my job in the City. Anytime I came back to visit my parents, it was for a weekend, and I rarely left the house.

"So, how long are you going to hide out at Mom and Dad's?" Dalton asks when we're a mile away from the house.

"I'm not hiding."

He laughs and shakes his head. "You're hiding."

"I needed help with work." I shrug. "Mom can help."

"Until February then?"

"No." But his suggestion doesn't sound half bad. "I don't know, D. I just needed to get away."

"Okay, tell me why. Mom didn't say much other than he broke your heart."

"His ex came back and she's pregnant. They were together for a long time, and once you see her, you realize I don't belong in the glitz and glam world that he's used to. It's easier for me to remove myself from the narrative."

"Are you planning to go back, Kelsey?" he asks as he turns the corner and pulls into a parking spot in front of the general store. I look out the window and sigh.

"Some things never change," I mutter.

"Small towns never want to change." Dalton helps me out of the car, and we make our way to the hardware store.

"Well as I live in breath if it isn't little Kelsey Sloane," Mr. Hanley says as we walk into the store. He comes around the corner and gives me a hug.

"Hello, Mr. Hanley, it's nice to see you."

"How is that rainy place you moved to treating you?"

"It's nice, but it's not New York."

"Nothing ever is." Mr. Hanley gives me another hug and then goes to help a customer.

I linger near the front and wait for Dalton, looking at the odds and ends of Mr. Hanley stocks. When the door opens, I don't look to see who it is. I figure if I avoid eye contact, no one will want to talk to me.

"No way."

It's been years since I've seen Tanner Pritchard. After our freshman year in college, he went on a road trip and never returned. He got to Texas and never left. That was the end of our three-year relationship.

I turn slowly and smile when our eyes meet. "Hey, Tanner."

"Wow, it *is* my Kelsey." We hug and it feels familiar. I didn't expect this feeling. We haven't seen each other in years. "I heard you're dating some pro football player?"

"Nah," I say, playing it off. "He's a client and took pity on me and showed me around Portland." This is easier than telling my old ex that my current ex broke my heart into a thousand pieces, and I could've prevented all of it by rebuffing his advances. He also doesn't need to know why Alex broke my heart.

"Well, I'll have to send him a thank you card for taking care of my girl."

*I am so not your girl anymore.*

"So, what's new?" I ask.

"Well, I got married, had a kid, and now I'm divorced. I moved to Rochester over the summer so my daughter can be closer to my parents. Her mom . . ." Tanner trails off.

I put my hand on his arm. "It's okay, you don't need to fill me in. I'm just happy to hear you're doing well."

"We should grab dinner while you're here. Maybe I can convince you to stay."

"Sure." Although, I'm not positive I want to grab dinner. Nothing against Tanner, but the last thing I want to do is fall back into old habits. They were hard to kick the first time around.

"Are you staying with your parents?"

I nod. Where else would I be?

"Let me see your cell phone. I'll give you my number."

I reach for my back pocket, only to realize my phone isn't in it. "Oh crap, I think I must've left it in Dalton's car or it's at the house. I just got in this morning, I'm a little out of sorts, and actually tired now that I think about it."

"No worries, I'll text your brother." Tanner puts his phone away. "I don't mean to pry but did someone hurt you?" he motions toward my arm.

I hold my cast up. "Nope. I tripped and fell. It's a small fracture, but enough of a nuisance that I came home to get help from my mom."

Dalton comes up to us with a bag of supplies. He and Tanner shake hands, and then Tanner tells him he's going to text him later to make plans with his sister. They laugh, thinking it's funny, when it's not. They did this kind of shit when we were in high school. Dalton and my other brother Davy think they can decide who I date.

Not that I plan to date Tanner.

We finally part and I head back to the car. I get in and sigh heavily and then groan. Dalton's laughing.

"Why don't you tell him no?"

"It's not that easy," I tell him. "If you had a high school romance resurface, it would be the same for you."

Dalton scoffs. "She pops up all the time."

"Really?"

He nods. "Sophie's in Buffalo. She's single and I see her all the time."

"Are you guys back together?"

He chuckles. "Hell no. But she has an itch, so I scratch it. It's a safety thing. We have a good time together, we have zero expectations of each other, and we're good in bed. It's easy."

"Dalton, that's horrible. She probably wants more."

Dalton side eyes me. "Or I want something more and she doesn't. Sophie went through a bad divorce. She has two kids and splits custody. I still haven't met her kids but want to. Her ex, he's not a good guy."

"Great," I mumble. My brother is going to end up being on some episode on Dateline because his girlfriend's ex went crazy. "Does Mom know?"

"Nope, and I'd like to keep it that way."

We don't talk much until we pull into the driveway. "Looks like Tanner has something else to say."

"Why do you . . ." I turn around and see his truck parked behind us. "Great."

Dalton giggles. "I bet he called, and Mom invited him over."

"Shoot me, now."

Tanner gets out of his truck and runs to open the door for me. "I didn't want to wait to see you again."

I'm at a loss for words. I smile and ignore his offered hand to help me out of the car. The last thing I want to do is be rude, but I also have no intentions of rekindling a college romance that ended when I was nineteen.

## TWENTY-FOUR

## ALEX

I hate my reflection. The man staring back at me is a man I don't want to know or even be. I'm angry, sad, and frustrated. And I blame Maggie. I've never been so mad at someone in my life, until now. The level of agitation I feel for her is nothing I've ever experienced before. The mere mention of her name or even seeing her name on my phone display, sends me into a downward spiral.

Before, when she left for London, I had hope. I thought we'd end up back together. Yeah, I secretly wished her job wouldn't work out. Was it wrong of me? Sure. But at the time she had broken my heart, and I missed her. When she came back for a visit, I turned on the charm. I wanted her to stay. Looking back, falling back into bed with her was a mistake. Obviously, hindsight and all that shit. Deep down, I knew she had no intentions of returning.

Until now.

Seeing her at my front door ruined my life.

It took meeting and falling for Kelsey to realize my relationship with Maggie wasn't real. I can't be me when

I'm with her. She wants me to be her picture-perfect man, with perfectly coiffed hair, wearing a suit and tie everywhere we go, and always ready for a photo-op. She used me, for whatever that's worth. Which makes zero sense to me. Why not go after Julius or Cameron, someone who is always the talk of the media? Not the center, whose sole purpose is to put the ball into the quarterback's hands. I am not popular in the realm of other position players. Hell, until Maggie, no one even knew what I looked like.

She changed me.

"She turned you into a charity project," I say to my reflection as I set the barbell down. I shouldn't lift weights if my mind isn't clear. This is how people get hurt.

My teammates linger around me. Some run on the treadmill while others lift. A few of the guys are working on their core with a yoga instructor. I tried that shit once, but she went so fast for a "beginners" class I gave up. It's still on my list of things to add to my off-season workout though.

Noah walks behind me and makes a funny face in the mirror to get me to laugh. He knows what's going on since he was my emergency, I'm too drunk to drive, phone call. Instead of taking me home, he sat with me for another couple of hours while I spilled my guts. He'd been in a similar situation with his ex. She knew he was in love with Peyton and told Noah she was pregnant. He stayed with her, breaking his and Peyton's heart in the process, only to find out his ex had told people she'd slept with Noah's dad, and he was the father of her baby. This mess almost cost Noah his career, and he might have quit if it wasn't for Peyton.

He pats me on the back. "It gets better."

"When?"

Noah shakes his head slightly. "I don't know, man. But

it does. Peyton says if Kelsey's the one for you, you guys will find your way back to each other."

"Your wife's a hopeless romantic." I'm not even mad he told her. He's very clear about how he shares everything with his wife.

He chuckles. "I love that about her." He pauses and looks around the room. "Come on, let's go outside. It's too nice to be in here." Except outside is an indoor football field because it's not nice outside right now. It's in the thirties and raining. But it's better than being in the stuffy gym, staring at myself.

I grab the bin of balls and drag it out to the field and wait for Noah to give me some instructions.

"I want to throw," he says.

"Um . . . okay? What about Julius?"

"Nah, just us for right now."

"And me." Peyton's voice echoes through the facility. She comes over with her clipboard and sits down near the bin of balls.

"You messed up, didn't you?" I ask Noah. I look from him to his wife and shake my head.

Peyton smiles. "He didn't. I just like watching him."

"You're not going to get all lovey-dovey on me, are you?" I ask the boss lady.

She shrugs and keeps her eyes on her husband. That right there, is the kind of love I want, and the kind I know I'd have with Kelsey if given the chance.

I run off and grab an empty bin and then head down field, ready to catch whatever Noah throws my way. Only that's a lie because I can't catch shit which is probably why I'm a center and not some hot shot QB or receiver. I can tackle, block, and make sure my quarterback has the ball in his hands on time.

I jump up and down and roll my shoulders to get ready. My eyes bug out when Noah hands Peyton the ball. All right, I get it. I take a couple steps in, and by a couple I mean I start to walk toward her.

"I'd stop if I were you," Noah says.

"Really?"

"Or not."

Peyton goes through the motions of receiving the ball, drops back and fires a cannon downfield. The ball whizzes by my ear and I'm too stunned to even try and catch it.

"Alrighty then," I mumble to myself and head back to the bin.

She does it again and again, until she's thrown every ball my way. I've caught maybe half, if that, and it's not because she's missed her target, it's because I can't catch worth a shit.

After picking up my dropped balls, I take the bin back to her and Noah. "Okay, what in the hell was that?"

Peyton shrugs.

When you want to give her a compliment, she's shy and modest. When she wants to point out where you failed during a game, she's a firecracker. I glance at Noah, who's beaming from ear to ear.

"When we were kids, she came to all my practices. Her father and my stepdad let her play. They treated her like one of the boys, and most of the time she was better than kids four to five years older than her."

I high-five Peyton and tell her I'll be her center every time.

"Hey, you're mine!" Noah says.

"Yeah, but she can throw better."

Peyton giggles, rises on her toes, and kisses Noah. "I love you. See you later."

"Bye, sweetheart." I call out when she starts to leave. She turns and gives me a little wave before turning back around. Noah watches her like a hawk until she's out of sight.

"You guys are relationship goals."

"I think it's different when you find the one you're meant to be with at an early age."

"You could've gone to jail."

"Nope, I waited until she was eighteen. What I could've done was destroy our families, but they all knew we were meant to be together."

"How did you know?"

"She's all I thought about. Hell, she's all I think about, even when she's next to me. Peyton's my obsession and I'd give up everything for her."

"When you say shit like that, it makes me feel like I don't love hard enough or I'm still searching for the right person for me."

Noah spins the football in his hands. "First off, don't compare your relationships with what Peyton and I have. I've known her since the day she was born. We grew up together and have always had this bond. I've loved her my entire life. Secondly, everyone feels different. My dad loved my mom, but he left. He pursued a career. Sometimes people need a break to realize what they're missing or what they want."

"What if she doesn't want me?"

"Peyton only wants me," he says as he tosses the ball at me.

I frown and toss it into the bin. We're not allowed to throw anything at Noah. "I'd never make a play for your wife. Ever. And you know I'm talking about Kelsey. What if I blew my chance with her?"

"Then wait. If she's meant to be with you, it'll happen. If not, you move on. You can't stress yourself out over something you can't change."

"And Maggie?"

"DNA test. She told you herself that she was with someone else. You have every right to keep her at arm's length until you know."

"Let me ask you this—had Dessie's baby been yours would you have married her?"

Noah thinks for a minute and nods. "Unfortunately, but I also think I would've cheated on her. Peyton's accident changed my life. It opened my eyes to what was right in front of me and once I stopped caring about what people thought, I went for what I wanted. Our families be damned."

We stop for the day and head into the locker room. I shower, dress and head out to my truck. My phone rings and Maggie's name shows up on the screen. I've avoided her as much as I can.

"Hey," I say as I answer and climb into my truck, instantly missing Kelsey. The cab still smells like her perfume, although it's starting to fade.

"I'm organizing a fundraiser for the hospital and I'm thinking of doing the auction again. I am going to put you down on the list."

"No," I say before I realize it's out of my mouth.

"What?"

I sigh and pinch the bridge of my nose. "I can't be that person . . . your person anymore, Maggie."

"Excuse me?"

"You heard me. I want the DNA test done, now. I don't want to wait any longer. It's not fair and this situation you've put me in is hurting Kelsey."

"I thought you weren't speaking to her anymore."

"It doesn't matter. Me and this other guy, we deserve to know now, not after the baby comes. If he's the father, he has a right to bond with his newborn and all that shit."

"Well, I need your support right now," she says.

"And I need you to schedule this today. As far as your fundraiser, go through the proper channels. You can use the team or call my agent."

"I can't believe you're being like this, Alex. After everything."

"Yep, I know." I hang up and bang my head against my steering wheel. There isn't a doubt in my mind that what I said to her was terrible, but it's the only way I can get through to her. If I continue to let her control my life, it's never going to end.

While I'm throwing my pity party, my phone dings with a new email. I check and find that it's from Russ, Kelsey's colleague, about my children's book—the book I wanted to write as an excuse to be near Kelsey.

The only line that stands out is, "I'll be taking over this project."

Kelsey is eliminating me from all aspects of her life.

I don't know what to think, but I know how I feel. My already fragile heart is shattering once again. It's like she's walking out of my life for good, and I don't like this one bit. Instead of replying, I call Kelsey.

Five rings and my call goes to voicemail.

I hang up and press her name again.

This time, it's voicemail right away. She sent me there.

The sound of her voice brings tears to my eyes. I miss her. "Hey, Kels, it's me. I got an email from Russ just now. I'm shocked, but I'm also hurt. I'm not interested in doing this project unless it's with you, so I don't know where to go from here. Hell, I don't know where to go at all. I miss you, honey. I love you. Please call me so we can talk. Please."

The system cuts me off before I can make a bigger fool of myself. I stay there in the parking lot, waiting for her to call back.

A call that never comes.

# TWENTY-FIVE

# KELSEY

Every morning, my mom and I sit down at the kitchen table and work. I print the current manuscript I'm working on twice, and while I read, I tell Mom what to mark. It's cute seeing her focus on making sure the proofing marks are correct, and it's comical when we come to a sex scene. The amount of "oh, Gods" I've heard (and read) has reached an all-new threshold. Still, with her impeccable handwriting, she makes meticulous notes for me, which I appreciate. I'm not sure what I'd accomplish if I were in Portland. Besides, Alex is there and he's persistent. I'd worry too much about whether he'd try and see me at work or home.

Halfway through my day, I receive an email from my old employer. They heard I was in town—and while I may be in the state, I'm nowhere near the city—and wanted to see if I'm interested in interviewing with them for a supervisory role. The position would mean more money than I make now and standard hours. No more long hours at home or working on the weekends to edit.

"Sounds interesting," my mom says when I read her the email. "What do you think?"

"I like the idea of more money for sure, but I do love my job as an editor. It's what I went to school for."

"Advancement is good for a career though," she says. "They reached out to you for a reason. I would interview for it. You have nothing to lose. Besides, you could start a family with those hours."

"Mom!" I roll my eyes at her. She's desperate to be a grandparent and neither of my brothers are close to settling down. Well, except for Dalton, but mom doesn't know he's been seeing Sophie, and I'm not sure his every other week, or whenever he's in town, and convenient hook-up is moving toward a full-fledged relationship.

What do I know though. I'm definitely not one to offer advice on anything love related. I'm in love with a man who may or may not be having a baby with a former girlfriend he's clearly not over.

*What a fool I am.*

"You should interview."

"Why?" I ask her.

She stands and goes to the kitchen, returning with the pot of coffee. After filling our mugs, she sits back down. "I'd love to have you in the same time zone. I know I'm selfish in saying this, but having you so far away, it hurts. A couple weeks back I randomly said to your dad, 'Let's go see Kelsey this weekend' except it's not that easy. I can't just get in the car and be there by dinner. Seeing you takes planning, and I'm not used to it. And before you bring up Davy living in Florida, I say the same thing to him. I send him job postings all the time. I get that where your father and I decided to live isn't necessarily for you, but that doesn't mean I don't want my babies close to me."

"Ah, Mom. You love us."

"Only sometimes." She smirks. "Anyway, I'm not trying to pressure you into making a decision one way or the other, it's an interview, and those never hurt anyone."

She's right. If anything, it gives me experience and maybe a bargaining tool later on if I want a promotion with Willamette Publishing. Knowing my former employer wants me back though is a really gratifying feeling. It shows they miss me and makes me wonder if I made a mistake in moving across the country.

As if the universe knows this is going to be a struggle, two text messages pop up on my phone.

ALEX MOORE

Hey, Kels. I just wanted to let you know I miss you.

TANNER PRITCHARD

Lunch today?

"What's wrong?"

How does she know?

I set my phone down and shake my head. "Alex misses me, and Tanner wants to have lunch."

"Oh boy, it's a good thing Alex isn't here or one of them might want to pee on you."

"Gross. You definitely needed more girls in your life," I tell her. "You talk like Davy."

Mom snorts out a laugh. "I can't help it." She eyes my phone. "What are you going to do?"

I look at it and sigh. "I don't know. Alex . . ." Another sigh and the threat of tears make me pause. "I love him. I fell hard and fast. Of course, I never told him because he's this larger than life pro athlete and I thought there's no way in hell he'd want to be with mousy little me."

"You're anything but mousy, Kelsey."

"I'm his little spoon," I say quietly. "And then I run into Tanner."

"He's been through a lot," mom says. "His daughter is adorable."

"That might be the case, but he left me, remember?" I remind her. "We'd made plans and he just took this road trip and decided to stay in Texas. He didn't even ask if I wanted to join him. He just left. It was as if he forgot about me."

"I'm sure that wasn't the case."

"You're right. He probably met the woman that became his wife." I had always thought Tanner cheated, but never wanted to believe it. Now, I think my suspicions were right. But do I care? I'm not sure I do. Alex may have withheld the truth about his relationship with Maggie, but there isn't a doubt in my mind that Tanner was unfaithful to me.

"Well, I can't argue with that," Mom says. "And Alex?"

"His ex is pregnant. The last thing he told me was he didn't know if the baby was his or not, which is why I've stepped away," I tell her. "I was under the impression they hadn't seen each other in a while but she was in Portland a few months before we met, and they hooked up. He didn't tell me, not that he had to, until she showed up again on his doorstep."

"Did he know?"

I shake my head. "No, he didn't. He was pretty shaken up and nervous about it. He says things don't have to change but if the baby is his, I don't want to be the reason his or her parents aren't together."

"While I commend you for saying that, you're assuming Alex wants to be with his ex."

"I know. And I know it's wrong to assume he does, but I can't help the history there. And with a baby now in the mix, I feel squeezed out. His fans love her, the team loves her. I'm the outlier in the equation."

My mom pats my hand. "I think you're being too hard on yourself. You have a lot to offer someone whether it's Alex, Tanner, or someone else."

"Tanner isn't an option, Mom. I know you and Dad like him, but I have zero thoughts on rekindling anything with him. Besides, how can I justify being with him and not Alex? And I love Alex."

"Then why are you here?"

"Because my heart is broken and he's very much part of my life in Portland."

I NEVER TEXT TANNER BACK, but that doesn't stop him from showing up at my parents in time to watch the football game on Sunday. I don't know whose bright idea it was to watch the Pioneers, but they're on the big screen and my mom has made a ton of appetizers. I don't know what she's playing at, whether she wants me to see Alex on television or spend time with Tanner. Either way, I'm not a fan.

Tanner kisses my cheek when he comes into the house. It's as if he's forgotten the handful of years we didn't talk, and I hated him. I suppose he doesn't know I hated him because we never hashed out his disappearance, and frankly it's too late now to bring up old memories.

Still, he sits by me and makes it seem like we're long-lost friends. I get that he lives here and sees my parents and Dalton regularly, but I'm not on that level of friendliness right now. I sit up when the camera pans the team and search for Alex. Dalton mentions something about Noah, but I ignore him. I didn't realize how much I wanted to see Alex until now.

When they show him, he doesn't look like himself. His helmet is off, and he looks . . . miserable. Nothing like the Alex I'm used to. Did I do that to him?

"Which one's your client?" Tanner asks.

He's not my client anymore because I quit on him, even though he refused to give up on me. I point to Alex before the camera pans to the other members of the team. "Alex Moore. He's writing a children's book on how to safely play football since there are so many concerns with concussions these days."

"Yeah, it's a pretty violent sport."

I ignore his comment and continue to look for another glimpse of Alex.

The next time I see him is during the coin toss, and it's only of his backside or a shot of his face with his helmet on. My heart double taps, reminding me that he's the man I'm in love with, that I fell hard for and want back. But at what cost? I don't know if I can take the public side of his life or the fact that his ex could be carrying his child. When there's a commercial, I excuse myself and go into the kitchen. Tanner follows.

"So, I'm thinking dinner tomorrow?" He sets his hands on the counter, caging me in. "I'm off work by five, I can pick you up at six. Maybe drive to Buffalo or this weekend, head to Niagara. Did you bring your passport?"

"Tanner . . ."

"You can decide later," he says, interrupting me. "You used to love it up there, and if we cross over, we can hit the casino, stay in the hotel."

"No." It comes out a bit more sharply than I intended, but it's enough that he steps back.

"Okay?"

I cover my face with my hand. "I'm sorry. I'm just going to be honest here, Tanner. It was great seeing you the other day, but nothing is going to happen between us. I'm not some hopeless romantic fictional character looking to rekindle a lost love. Maybe if our situation was different, but it's not. You left me without telling me why."

"I—"

I hold my hand up for him to stop. "Whatever the excuse was, it's in the past, and it's not going to change how I feel. The truth is, my client—that man on the television, I'm in love with him."

"Isn't that a conflict of interest?"

"Well, that's the thing, he used the excuse of wanting to write a book as a way to see me, but now he's with a different editor at my publishing house, so no, it's not. But that's beside the point." I sigh heavily. "I love him and I'm here, and he's there, and shit's complicated between us right now."

"Use me to uncomplicate things, then. I don't mind being a rebound. We loved each other once. It can happen again." He shrugs.

"No, Tanner. That's not how things work. If you know me at all, you know I'm not someone who uses people."

"We were good together, Kelsey."

"*Were* being the operative word there, Tanner."

"Game's on," Dalton yells.

"We should go and watch the game," I tell Tanner, who doesn't flinch. Standing there with him solidifies my decision on whether I want to interview with my former employer—I don't. I love my job in Portland and I love Alex. It's where I'm meant to be.

I excuse myself and head back into the living room and cheer for the Pioneers. Thankfully, they won, which has my brother begging for Super Bowl tickets if the Pioneers go again. I ignore him mostly because I would never ask Alex for such a thing.

When the game's over, I head to my bedroom and listen to the voicemail I saved from Alex, needing to hear his voice.

"*Hey, Kels, it's me, Alex. I don't know where you are right now, but you're not home and you're not at work. I'm worried. Please just let me know you're okay. Basha says you are, but I need to hear it from you. I love you, honey. More than I've shown you. I am so damned sorry for what I've put you through. Please call or text me. Just to say hi. That's all I need right now. No, that's a lie. I need you. Kels. So much.*"

I listen a couple of times before texting him.

> It's me, letting you know, I'm okay.

# TWENTY-SIX

## ALEX

Am I a winner or a loser? It's hard to say these days. My team's winning. We're number one in the league with three weeks left in the season. The target on our back is red and huge. Teams want to stop us, cut us down at the knees and make us bleed. Some call Noah cocky and he needs to be taught a lesson. Some say we're seeing what his dad would've done had he ever made it to the NFL. Others are trying to find a way onto our roster.

Me . . . I'm trying to make it to Sunday's game in San Diego. Ever since Kelsey has been gone, I've been in contact with Basha. It's really the only way to know if Kelsey's okay. It took some VIP seats, a meet and greet, and a dinner date with Cameron for her to agree to give me any information. I'm not ashamed to admit I would've thrown the world at Basha to get information out of her. I know Kelsey's been at her parents' in New York, and I also know her ex is sniffing around her, but I'm told I don't need to worry because she told him she's in love with me.

*She's in love with me.*

Until I hear her say those words, I won't let them sink in. But I sure as shit will let them linger in my mind because they give me hope. More hope than I've had in a long time.

More hope than I have right now, sitting next to Maggie, who sits next to the other man in her life. We shook hands when he walked in but didn't exchange names. I don't know him and he doesn't know me. I don't even know where he came from. London, maybe? It's not like we're going to be friends, and if I have my way, I'll never have to see him again after this.

Actually, I don't know if he's in Maggie's life or not, but I don't want to refer to him as the other man, because I'm not her man. At all. And I have zero intentions of being hers again. I've made myself very clear—if she's pregnant with my child, I'll be there for the child. I don't want to be with someone I'm not in love with.

The three of us wait in an office, which I feel is overkill. Why couldn't all of this be done with a phone call or a letter in the mail. This is what Maggie wanted—the dramatics of it all. Over the past few weeks, I've come to realize she loves the limelight and attention. The more dramatic, the better for her. I don't know how I didn't see it earlier, but it's clear as day now. What I also never knew is she wanted me to look a certain way. The Maggie Gardner way with styled hair, clean shaven, and always in a suit and tie. The dirty looks she's given me since I've walked in dressed in jeans and a hoodie, with a week's worth of facial hair is testament to what I've discovered.

All of this makes me miss Kelsey more. I mean, I *know* why she likes my gray sweatpants, but she never told me to change or shave. She never commented on whether I gelled my hair or not. She just wanted to be with me, and I allowed my stupidity around Maggie to mess that up.

Finally, the doctor or whoever it is we're waiting for comes in. She introduces herself but I don't bother to let her name register in my mind. I'm already on edge. Nervous. As much as I want to be a parent—someday—it's not with Maggie, and I don't want this to ruin my chances with Kelsey. I shake my head when that thought runs through my mind because it makes me feel like a selfish prick. Children are a gift. I know this much from being an uncle. This just isn't the ideal situation.

"I'll cut to the chase," the doctor says, with a beaming smile, as if this is fun. She looks at each of us.

"Can we get on with it?" I ask with a heavy sigh.

"This isn't Maury," Maggie says.

"Then why does it feel like that's exactly what we're doing?" I ask her. "I'm pretty damn sure that was your plan; bring us both onto national TV, yell and scream, and expect one of us to dance a jig when Maury says, 'you're not the father.'"

Maggie says nothing and tries to smile at the doctor.

"Can you tell me if I'm the father?" I ask the doctor.

"You're not," she says.

"Thank you." I stand and take large strides to exit the room, not waiting to hear if the other guy is the father or not. I'm not and that's all that matters. As soon as I'm in the parking garage I let out a huge bellow. People look at me oddly, but I don't care. They have no idea what I just went through.

On the way to my truck, I text Noah.

NOT MINE!

NOAH WESTBURY

Dude!

Congratulations

I'm sorry she put you through that.

Now what?

Now, I try to win Kelsey back.

I have a plan.

NOAH WESTBURY
Peyton says let us know if we can help.

I will

And thanks for being my friend.

I really needed it these past few weeks.

NOAH WESTBURY
That's what I'm here for.

I want to tell Kelsey, but something like this has to be done in person. When I say those words to her, I want to see her expression when they sink in for her. I'm barely in my truck when Maggie and her friend come into the parking garage. I'm not even tempted to know the results and pull out of my spot just as they pass by. I can't tell if either of them are happy or not. For all I know, she wants him to be her baby's father, and I'm okay with it. What I'm not okay with is how she used me when she returned. Showing up at my house unexpectedly, like nothing has happened between us and acting like I didn't have a girlfriend, was wrong on so many levels. She's not the person I fell in love with years ago. This much is evident.

After paying my parking fee, I head to Cameron's to pick him up before we go to Willamette Publishing to take Basha to the airport. They've gone on a couple of dates, and

I can't really tell if they're into each other or not, but this is better than me having to hoist Basha into my truck. Clearly, I made the mistake of leaving Rizzo at home, as it would've made more sense to drive her today, but I hate being on the freeway with a small car like that. People drive like assholes until they see my truck. Then they're not so cocky in their Mercedes.

As soon as Basha exits the building Cameron jumps out and grabs her suitcase and puts it in the back. He helps her into the front seat and then climbs into the back.

"Do you have your tickets?" I ask her. She's on her way to San Diego for a conference and plans to stay an extra day to catch our game. Due to some weird weather pattern, it's going to be in the eighties all week down there and she wants to take advantage. Honestly, I don't blame her. I wish Coach took us down early.

Basha pats her bag. "I do, and everything's set."

"Perfect."

"Did you find out?" she asks.

"Not mine," I tell her as I eye Cameron through the rear-view mirror. Noah's the only one I've told, but people have seen Maggie at the games, and of course, her pregnancy hit the news wire with the headline being we're expecting. We're not. She is.

"That's the best news I've heard all day."

"Fuck that," I say. "It's the best news I've heard in a long time."

The three of us make idle chit chat, mostly about the things to do in San Diego. I haven't been, other than for games, but according to Cameron I really need to visit. Basha says the beaches are amazing down there, and she's definitely looking forward to the spa day she has booked.

When we get to the airport, Cameron jumps out to help

Basha with her things. "I'm going to walk her in," he says. "You should circle around."

"Sure." If I didn't owe Basha my life, I'd tell Cameron to fuck off because circling around Portland airport isn't exactly my idea of a good time. Still, I do as he asks because I'm a nice fucking guy and this will bring a smile to Basha's face.

Instead of circling, I leave the area and park off to the side at the nearest cell phone lot. I text Cameron to let him know where I am and to just let me know when he's ready to come get him. Airport romance—I'm sure that's a book somewhere, and if not, maybe Kelsey needs to ask one of her authors to write it for her.

While I wait for Cameron, I look through the photos of Kelsey on my phone, only for Maggie to interrupt me.

MAGGIE GARDNER

You were very rude in the office today.

I think about not responding but fuck that.

> I don't care. This whole thing has fucked with my life. You could've told me long before you showed up at my door that you were pregnant, so I could've been prepared. Instead, you waltzed back into my life like you never left knowing I had a girlfriend. You didn't give a rat's ass about her feelings so I don't care about yours right now, Maggie.

MAGGIE GARDNER

I've said I'm sorry. I didn't know where else to go.

Do you want me to talk to Kelsey? I will.

> No, I don't. You've made things bad enough for me where she's concerned. Nothing you can say or do will change the damage done.

MAGGIE GARDNER

> If you change your mind

> I won't.

I've never said a mean thing to her in my life until recently. It's like her head is stuck in the clouds. She only cares about herself. If I didn't need to go back and pick Cameron up, I'd turn my phone off. Thankfully, Maggie stops texting, but I'm sure it's only a matter of time before she hits me up for something else.

Finally, Cameron texts me and I circle back to pick him up. He gets into the truck and says, "I like Basha, but I'm not sure if it'll work."

"Ha, why's that?"

"She's not a football fan."

"What are you talking about?"

Cameron shakes his head. "She's a fan of tight pants."

I can't help but laugh. "I think she's messing with you. She's a version of Peyton. Basha knows a lot of random facts about the game. Shit I didn't even know."

He eyes me suspiciously. "The last thing she said to me as she slapped my ass was 'don't forget to bend over for me.'"

I laugh so hard I swerve and almost hit the guardrail.

"Of course, if you kill us before the game, I won't be under pressure to keep bending over in front of the stands."

"Yeah, sorry man. She's hilarious, and I think she likes teasing you."

"Yeah," he says with an exasperated sigh. "She's funny all right."

We make our way back into town, stopping at the mall first, which turns into a massive autograph session. As soon as some young boy sees us, he asks for a picture and then for us to sign his shirt, which we happily do. The only problem is when one sees you, the rest come in hoards, and they don't stop. They follow you to the store and wait until you make eye contact with them before they ask.

By the time we get what we need and make it back to my truck, a thirty-minute jaunt to the mall has turned into three hours.

"Are you going to feed me?" Cameron asks.

"I'm not your bitch," I tell him.

"True, but if it wasn't for me, you would've had to touch Basha's ass to get her into your truck and Kelsey would've found out and you'd be in more hot water. I saved your ass."

"How's Italian?"

"Sounds good to me."

## TWENTY-SEVEN

## KELSEY

The day before I leave my parents, my mom throws me a goodbye party. I think this is her way of showing me how much she'll miss me. Coming home has been cathartic. I needed the time away from Portland and away from Alex to really grasp what I want out of life.

Now I know.

It's Portland. I fell in love with the city, my job, and my coworkers. I miss them.

It's also Alex and even if he doesn't want me, he's the bonus that comes with being there. Are we the perfect couple? No, we're not. We're a work in progress that needs editing. But I'm willing to put in the time to get us to a place where we both want to be.

Tanner came over one last time to say goodbye and plead his case. He wants a second chance to make things right and I tell him he can do that by being my friend, and it would be unfair of me to be with him when my heart belongs to another.

Dalton drives me to the airport. He volunteered

because then he can see his ex. He tells me they're not getting back together, but then when I question why he's letting this fling go on longer than it should, he doesn't have a response. He hugs me when we arrive at security and tells me he's going to try and come out for a visit. I think he'd like it out there.

I'm on a flight to San Diego to meet up with Basha for the writer's conference and sit next to the window with the shade up most of the time, even though the sun is bright and shines through. It's nice to see and I swear I feel the temperature shift when we reach the southwest corner of the country. They're experiencing a winter heatwave which is such an oxymoron.

After landing, I work my way to baggage and the fee for the cart, wishing my brother was with me to do all of this for me. I glance at my arm and my highly decorated with signatures and doodles cast and groan. I'm ready for this thing to come off. My arm itches and I'm tired of wrapping it in plastic to take a shower.

With my luggage on the cart, I push it outside and get in line for a taxi. This has to be the worst part of traveling to a location where you don't know anyone. Thankfully, the line moves rather quickly and before I know it, we're speeding away. The closer we get to the hotel, the heavier the traffic becomes.

"Lots going on in town," the driver says.

"Like what?"

"Many conventions. Football. Military celebration."

*Football.* As much as I want to forget Alex and I are in the same city, I can't. It'll be odd, being here while he's here, and not seeing him until I get back to Portland. We haven't spoken since the day of my accident, aside from a couple of text messages to each other, and I didn't want to be like "Hey, I'm in town, hook me up with tickets."

"Sounds like it's going to be a great economic boost for San Diego."

"We appreciate it," the driver says. He pulls into the valet of the hotel, which is connected to the center where our writers conference is. While I process the payment, he gets my bags out of the trunk and hands them to one of the bellhops there.

"Thank you," I tell him as I hand him a cash tip.

"Enjoy your stay."

After I check in, I tell the bellhop which room I'm staying in and send Basha a text to say I'm on my way up. After a quick elevator ride, Basha's squealing and hugging me.

"I've missed the hell out of you."

"We saw each other every day."

"Video chat doesn't count."

"Yeah, you're right." I tip the bellhop and then flop back on the bed.

"Nope, get up and come see this view." Basha tugs on my good arm and pulls me toward the window. We have a view of the pool area. The large pool is split into two, with one side being sandy and the other like any other pool. There are very few people down there.

"It looks magical."

"Do you want to go down there? Since it's a weekday, we don't need a reservation."

"I should really work."

"I should too, but we can do that while we're down there. Come on, change and we'll head down."

The offer is too good to pass up. We change into our

swimsuits, and I put on a summer dress as a cover up. I had to dig deep in my closet back at my parents to find some summer clothes for this trip. I wasn't expecting such high temperatures, but this abnormal heatwave is definitely welcome.

Basha gives the young man at the booth our room number. He tells us where we can find towels and when he sees our laptops, tells us where we can find outlets if we need them.

"He's cute," Basha says, earning an eye roll from me. She's smitten with Cameron Simmons, even though she confided in me that she only sees him as a friend. Nothing wrong with having friends in your life, that's for sure.

If Alex and I can't find our way back to each other, I hope we at least end up being friends. Although, I know that can be tricky. Once you cross the line from friends to lovers, it's hard to go back, especially when there are feelings there. He may not want to put up with my insecurities though. Why would someone, who could literally have anyone, want to put up with someone second-guessing him and their relationship all the time?

Basha and I find a couple of chaises and spread out. With the stupid cast still on, I'm limited, but am able to read. Before I left my parents, I printed out all the submissions authors have sent for their fifteen minutes with me this weekend. They're going to pitch their story, and I need to figure out in that time slot if we want to continue talking or not. It's like speed dating for editors and authors.

At some point, Basha and I order lunch, including some cocktails, and reapply our sunscreen. I write as many questions as I can on the manuscripts in illegible handwriting and wish this damn cast was off. I should've made an appointment at the doctor's office in Buffalo and had it removed. But no, I'm a good patient and listened to the doctor in Portland. My arm feels totally fine . . . *famous last words.*

AT THE END of the conference, the keynote speaker congratulates everyone on a successful weekend. I met with over thirty authors and have asked for full manuscripts from twelve of them. I'll be grateful if I get six signed to a contract. I call that success, except for the challenge of getting them on the books with release dates.

Basha and I have a spa day today. She booked us for massages at an off-site location. We stand outside, in the heat, waiting for our rideshare to show up when a black limo stops in front of the valet.

"Who do you think that is?" I ask.

She shrugs. "Lifestyles of the rich and famous," she sighs. "What I wouldn't give to ride around town in that."

"Same," I say.

The driver steps out and comes toward us. "Kelsey Sloane?"

I swallow hard, look at Basha, who focuses on the car, and then I look at the driver. "Uh . . . yes?"

"Come with me, please."

He motions for me to walk ahead, but my feet are firmly cemented to the ground. Basha nudges me forward and my steps falter. "What is this?"

The driver holds the rear door open. I peek inside and see Pioneer gear sitting on the seats. "Courtesy of Mr. Moore."

"Excuse me?"

"Get in the car, Kelsey," Basha says.

"What's going on?"

Basha expression changes from indifference to elation. "Alex is trying to win you back. Now get in the car before I have to shove you in."

"Did you do this?" I ask her.

"No, it's all Alex. I'm just the go between. Now get in. The game starts soon and there's going to be traffic. We can't be late."

I look around for Alex. Is he hiding somewhere? The thought of him near sends ripples through my body. My heart wants him. It craves his presence. I don't see him but still hesitate before climbing into the back. Once I get in, Basha's right behind me. As soon as the door closes, she puts one of the jerseys over her shirt, puts the foam finger on her hand, and opens the moonroof. Before I can even register what she's doing Basha stands up through the window.

"Basha!"

"Woohoo, let's go Pioneers!"

Should I be embarrassed?

No, I shouldn't. I put my jersey on and follow Basha. I pound on the top of the car and match her enthusiasm. The only reason I'm a football fan is because of Alex, and if he did this for me, then I'm going to make sure every damn person on the street and in the parking lot of the stadium knows we're here for the Pioneers.

Basha takes two passes out of her fanny pack and hands them to the person at the gate. "When did you do all of this?" I ask her.

"Like I said, it was all Alex. He's been pretty distraught since you left and asked me to help."

"Help with what exactly?"

"Nothing too much. The Pioneers just happened to be

in town while we are here. Don't look deep into it. Alex got us tickets."

"And sent a limo, with gear. There's more going on here."

Basha says nothing as we make our way to our seats. As luck would have it, we're right on the railing, behind the team. I know these seats must've cost Alex a fortune because they're definitely not the seats most of the wives and girlfriends sit in. She pauses when we get to our row and motions for me to go in. My mouth drops open when I see who's sitting in there.

"Surely, we must have the wrong seats."

"Nope," Basha says. "However, I'm under strict orders that I have to sit on the end."

"Fuck my life," I mutter under my breath to her. As if my legs are made gelatin, I take one wobbly step after another until a certain set of eyes looks up at me. And then he smiles, and everything in me just turns to mush.

"Hey, Kelsey."

Holy fuck Liam Page remembers my name.

"Uh . . . h-hi."

"Hey, Kelsey." Harrison James taps me on the shoulder. He waves, as does his partner, who's holding a toddler in her lap. And then next to her, is the rest of their family.

"This can't be my life right now."

Next to Liam, his wife leans forward and waves. "Noah told us you work in books."

I nod because forming a coherent sentence right now is impossible.

"Great, maybe after the game you can give me some recommendations."

Again, another nod.

Basha pushes me into my seat, but I'm only there for a

moment when Alex approaches the wall. He beckons me to him, and I go, showing security my pass when I get to the bottom of the stairs. Alex is there, on the other side of the gate, looking at me with such anticipation and love.

As soon as I'm within arm's reach, he pulls me to him. The hug is awkward and bulky because of his pads, but I don't care. It feels good being near him. I should pull away, but I don't want to. Not anymore. I'm tired of fighting what my heart desires. It's him. We have a lot of unresolved conflicts, but we'll figure it out. One way or the other.

"I'm glad you're here."

"I'm having an out of body experience right now."

He chuckles and kisses the top of my head.

I step back and look everywhere but at Alex. He tips my chin, forcing me to look at him. I expect him to say something, but instead he leans forward and presses his lips to mine. Over the noise level, I hear Basha cheer us on. I pull away and hide my face in his jersey.

Alex turns his back so the people in the stadium can't see us. "I love you, Kels. Tell me what I have to do for a second chance?"

"There isn't anything you need to do except we need to talk. I don't like that you kept the hook-up from me, But I'm yours, Alex. I'm here."

He scoops me up and twirls me around. "Thank fuck. I've been miserable without you, and I promise to never ever let my stupidity come between us again."

"Me too," I tell him honestly. "I've hated being away from you and only being able to see you on television. But this situation with Maggie—"

Alex smiles brightly and refuses to let me down. "There's no situation," he interrupts me. "The baby isn't mine. And you'll never know how sorry I am for not coming clean about her earlier visit. I'm sorry I hurt you in that way."

I don't know how to measure relief, but I'm flooded with it. I probably shouldn't be happy, but I am. So fucking happy.

Alex finally puts me down, even though I'd be content staying in his arms. "I don't know what to say," I tell him. "Are you sad?"

"She's not the one I want to start a family with."

"No?"

He shakes his head. "You are, when we're ready."

"Me?" I ask, dumbfounded.

"Of course," he says. He steps forward and cups my cheek and then leans down. "This is a conversation for another day, Kels. But I, for one, can't wait to start practicing again."

My body shivers, and he kisses my cheek. "Go sit with the band, honey. They're expecting you. I'll see you after the game."

"I love you, Alex. Kick some ass today!"

"Anything for you."

## TWENTY-EIGHT

## ALEX

From an outsider's point of view, Kelsey and I kissed and made up. The truth is relationships are hard work. This is something I've learned from dating Kelsey to the situation with Maggie, to getting back together with Kels. I used to take everything with an easy come, easy go attitude. But that attitude is what got me into trouble with Kelsey. My lifestyle isn't easy to take, and I thrust her into it, thinking she was like Maggie. I forgot Maggie was new to the attention and used to get nervous on dates, just the same as Kelsey is now. It was wrong of me to think I had the ebb and flow mastered.

I'm not sure I ever will, but I sure as hell am trying.

Doing what I did at the game in San Diego was probably the easiest and hardest thing I had ever done. I knew where I wanted Kelsey to sit, so I could flirt with her throughout the game, but knowing 4225 West sat there had me second guessing my plan. Thankfully, Noah pulled some strings and helped me. He didn't have to ask his dad or Peyton's to help, but he did and did so without reservation.

Noah's a good friend and I'm damn lucky to have him in my life. I don't even know how I'll ever thank him, Liam, or Harrison for making Kelsey feel welcome and included, but I'm going to spend the rest of my life trying to find a way. The words aren't enough, and I'm not sure anything ever will be.

By the end of the game, Liam and Harrison had Kelsey laughing, taking selfies, and smiling so damn big. Of course, I knew some of that smile of hers was meant for me, and it felt good seeing her happy. That's how I want to see her, every day, for the rest of her life.

I stand in front of the mirror in my walk-in closet and adjust my bowtie. Behind, Kelsey fusses with her heels and mutters a string of unpleasantries. I stare at her through the mirror and take her in before turning around.

"Honey, sit down." I move the pile of clothes off the bench and guide her to it, and then crouch down and help her slip her shoe on. Once her foot is incased, I kiss her ankle. But that's not enough for me and I continue to move my way up her leg, bunching her dress as I go.

"Alex." There's a hint of warning in her tone. Only a hint though. She hasn't told me to stop. When I reach her red lace thong, I nuzzle her. Her gasp is faint.

"So, fucking sweet." I run my nose over the lace covering her. "Can I taste you?"

"No," she says softly, teasing me as her fingers push into my head.

I smile and pull her panties aside, while my other arm wraps around her waist to pull her forward a bit. I need better access. Miraculously this gorgeous dress I bought her is now over her hips and her legs widen. She may have told me no, but did she really mean it?

My knuckle brushes against her slit, causing her to gasp. "Alex, we don't have time." She moans and my tongue says differently after I taste her.

"Fucking delicious." Another lick from her center to her clit. My teeth graze her sensitive bud before putting my mouth there. "God, I fucking love this pussy."

"She loves you too."

"She fucking better because she's mine."

As much as I want to stay buried between her legs, we have an obligation. After another lick with a little tease around her hole, I put her panties back and kiss my way down her leg until I'm at her bare foot, where I help slip her heel on.

I stand and my hard-on ends up at her eye level. Kelsey licks her lips and I growl. "Later." As much as it pains me to say that word, if I let her tug my zipper down and free my cock, we'll miss the fundraiser and Coach will have my hide. With my contract coming up soon, the last thing I need is to give him an excuse to not renew me. Of course, if Noah leaves, I may follow, depending on Kelsey. It's not really something we talk about because she loves her job. For all I know, I could end up staying in Portland til retirement, although I'm way too young for that.

Stepping away from her penetrating eyes, I go back to the mirror and make sure my bowtie is straight, and then I head into the bathroom. Kelsey follows and fixes her makeup even though she looks flawless. I kiss her and then rinse my mouth out even though I'd love nothing more than to keep the taste of her on my tongue, I wouldn't want to embarrass her if someone noticed and said something. I work with a bunch of jocks, they're crude and have no filters.

A horn honks outside and we gather our things. I drape Kelsey's bare shoulders with a shawl and hold the door for her. The event is downtown and is a fundraiser with the Marines for Toys for Tots. We'll likely see Maggie for the first time since Kelsey and I have gotten back together. My plan is to ignore her but if she comes up to us, I'll be cordial. People will be watching, and I don't need to give anyone any ammunition.

Renting a limo for the night means I can focus on my love. She sits next to me, with her knees touching mine. I hand her a flute of champagne and touch my glass to hers.

"To us," I say.

"To us."

By the time we get downtown, we've had two glasses, and she has to grip my arm for support. "Don't let go of me," she begs.

"Never."

The photographers yell my name, and Kelsey freezes. I don't know if she'll ever get used to this or not, but she's promised to try, and I've promised to make it as easy on her as possible. If at any time she doesn't want her photo taken at an event, we can use the rear entrance. What I can't stop are the people on the streets. She's taken to wearing sunglasses or a hat most of the time.

I slip my arm around her and kiss her temple softly. "Are we good?" I keep my voice low so only she can hear me. One word from her and we'll leave. She nods.

We pose, take a couple of steps, pose again, and take a few more steps. We do this until we're safely inside the grand ballroom of the hotel.

"This place is magical," Kelsey says. I happen to agree. Red ribbons and white lights adorn the entirety of the room.

In one corner, there's a massive Christmas tree, and in the other, a string quartet plays holiday music.

Right off, we see Peyton and Noah, and head to them. "The turnout is more than the organizers expected," Peyton says after we exchange pleasantries.

"Everyone comes out when it's time to help the kids at Christmas," Kelsey adds. "My boss paid for a table as well, and we donated a ton of books to the center."

"When does your book come out?" Noah asks me.

I shake my head and look at Kelsey. "Jonathan is playing around with a spring or summer release. He hasn't decided yet, but it's much sooner than planned. Originally it was going to be a year from now."

"A tour?" I ask. "This is the first you're mentioning it."

"Well, I'm not your editor. Russ is. It's his job."

I hate that she's not my editor, but I get it. She wanted to push as much of me aside as she could then. Russ is a great guy, but he's not my Kelsey, who is the only reason I ever thought about writing the book to begin with.

"Will you go on this tour with me?"

Kelsey nods. "Of course."

"What if I want to go?" Noah asks.

"I mean, I know we're lovers, but sometimes you have to stay home."

Peyton snorts. "I knew it!" She fake punches Noah in the arm. Instead of dodging her, he pulls her into his arms and whispers something into her ear. Within seconds, she's a completely different person. I have no idea what he said to her, but the way she shifts, and her demeanor changes, makes me wonder what his magic words are.

Maybe it's the way he loves her and she him or the fact that they grew up together. They just know what each other needs and when. It's something I'll have to ask him at practice this coming week. I like to think Kelsey looks at me the same way, more so when I whisper into her ear. Although, the only thing I seem to whisper are naughty thoughts.

For all I know, Noah's doing the same thing.

The four of us find our seats and are happy to see Julius and Autumn at our table. They look haggard. "Hey," Julius says when we sit down.

"Everything okay?" Peyton asks Autumn.

She yawns and nods. "The baby's teething and thinks in the middle of the night is the best time to let us know about it. We're taking shifts, but he wakes Reggie and Roxy up, so we have a bed full of squirrely arms and legs."

"I used to do that," Kelsey says. "There's a magic comfort that comes from sleeping with your mom. She's the only one who can cuddle away the pain."

"I agree," Peyton says. "Although Oliver is at the stage where everyone and everything is his, so if I try to hug my mom or dad, he butts in. What's funny is if my dad tries to even touch my mom, Oliver lets him know he's not allowed to do it."

"I met him at the game," Kelsey says. "He's adorable. Can I ask why there's such an age gap though?"

"Oliver isn't a James yet. My parents are adopting him," Peyton tells her. "He's been with my parents for a year."

"Oh, I heard your sister got married," Autumn says.

Peyton nods. "Yes, she and Ben got married in Beaumont while he was in the hospital."

"Wait, I know Ben," I interject. "Why was he in the hospital?"

Peyton looks at Noah, who then looks at me. "Remember when I shaved my head on Instagram live?"

I nod.

"Ben's got cancer. Well, he's clear of it at the moment. Quinn, Mack, and I didn't want Ben to feel alone, so we shaved our hair with him."

"Is that why you told me to make that donation to the testicular cancer charity?"

Noah nods. "Yeah, and thanks for doing that. Hopefully with the amount of money the team sent in, we're helping."

"Okay, well now I'm going to cry," Kelsey adds. "You guys are amazing to each other."

"It's one giant family," Julius adds. His words remind me that I still need to speak to Noah about his future plans. He's hinted that the Pioneers might not be it and I'd kind of like to know before my contract expires.

We eat dinner, and then the center for underprivileged kids brings all their kids in. Santa becomes the focal point and hands out a present to each child. It's fun watching them open them, and it makes me miss my niece and nephew. I haven't spent a holiday with them in a while and I think I'm long overdue. Maybe next year, depending on the football schedule, I can plan a family getaway for mine and Kelsey's family. It's too late this year. Besides, I want to spend all my free time with Kelsey, just the two of us.

As the night winds down, we start to make our way outside. Thankfully, most of the media is gone, but there are a few stragglers hanging around, snapping photos of people coming out of the hotel and getting into cars. The limo that brought us, takes us home. It's a nice, relaxing drive, where I spend the majority of it staring at Kelsey. I'm so in love with her, it hurts sometimes. Even though I have her, I fear I'm going to lose her.

The limo drops us off and I follow Kelsey and stand

behind her while she puts the code to the front door. She opens the door, walks in and gasps.

Rose petals go from the front door to our Christmas tree, which is lit up in white. Soft music plays through the sound system, and the fireplace glows. Kelsey follows the path to the tree, where a lone present sits.

"What's this?" she asks of the medium sized box on the floor.

"Open it."

Kelsey tears the paper slowly, showing me how long it's going to take her to open the presents I bought her for the actual day. She opens the box, only to find another one.

"Alex."

I shrug. Sometimes jokes are fun.

After the third box, she finally reaches the end. She pulls the black velvet box out and I drop to my knee. "I thought of a million and one ways to do this."

"Alex!" She gasps and covers her mouth. I take the box from her hand and take the ring out of the velvet cushion and reach for her left hand.

"I know we haven't been together long or even known each other long, but I'm a firm believer in when you know, you know, and I know. You're the one for me, Kelsey. I've known from the first day you stepped into our practice facility. When I drew the piece of paper with 'winner' written on it, I thought I would give whoever was there a quick run-down of the game, and then hightail it out of there, but then I saw you, and my world shifted."

I slip the ring onto her finger even though I haven't asked. "Kelsey Lynn Sloane, will you do me the honor of becoming my partner for the rest of our lives?" I look into her eyes and see tears. "Will you marry me, honey?"

Kelsey drops to her knees and holds my face in between

her hands. "Yes, Alex. Hell yes, I'll marry you." We kiss, which turns heated in no time. "Strip me naked here," she says against my mouth. "Show me how much you love me. Make love to me, Alex."

"With pleasure."

# EPILOGUE

Kelsey finds me swimming laps when she gets home from work. We still don't live together, at least not full-time because my location doesn't make the best sense for her. And we're both torn on what to do. We love my house, but we also love her apartment. Hers is quaint and cozy, and I love being there. But my house is perfect, with the pool, jetted tub, and indoor-outdoor living space. Kelsey's apartment is close to work, for both of us, but we love the privacy of my home. Needless to say, we're confused about where we should live as a couple. We've even thought about buying a new place. It doesn't make sense though. Most of the homes are a distance from her job, and if we already have her apartment, why find another one?

I swim to the edge and then climb out of the pool. I don't bother to dry off, mostly because I like the way Kelsey looks at me when I get out of the pool. She swallows hard as I approach her, with only one thing on my mind—her.

"Hi, Kels," I say as I lean down and kiss her. "I missed you today."

"I missed you," she says breathlessly. "I have a present for you."

Any other day, I'd take her to the house or at least under the patio to the outside living room, but she actually has a present for me. Without taking her eyes off mine, she squats down and picks up the wrapped gift.

"Open it."

Slowly, I take the bow off, undue the taped sides, and lift the lid off the box. My eyes widen when I see the book I wrote nestled in tissue paper.

"It's the first copy," she tells me. "They were delivered today, and Russ brought the first one to me."

I take my book out of the box and hold it in my hand. When I approached Kelsey about this, it was an excuse so I could see her, and she made all of this happen. Now that I'm holding it in my hands, this is the coolest thing I have ever done. Sure, I'm a pro football player and have the hottest and best fiancée and my life is pretty great, but this . . . this book that has my name on the cover is by far the most amazing thing I have ever done.

"Wow!"

"You know, it's not every day that I get to see my client's reaction when they get their copies. I kind of like seeing your reaction."

I sit down on the chaise and flip through the pages. The illustrator did a fantastic job, and the Pioneer colors really pop on the glossy pages. My fingers trail over the words in amazement.

"You know I never thought this would happen."

"Why not?" Kelsey asks.

Shrugging, I continue flipping through the pages. "I used this as a ploy to spend time with you, and now look at it."

"You did good," she tells me. "But there's more."

"There is?"

She nods. "Russ has you booked for a signing at the bookstore."

"No way?"

"Yep, and the children from the center all get a free copy."

"I really like that."

Kelsey sits next to me. "There's more."

"I'm not sure I can take anymore news," I tell her.

"The team will be with you. Russ took copies over to the Myles today, and he's going to make sure they each get a copy before next week's event."

I set my hand on her leg. "That's really great. Some of the guys don't live here though. Like Noah."

"He'll be here," she tells me. "Russ and Myles have been planning this for a bit, in preparation for your summer release."

"You guys thought of everything, didn't you?"

"It our jobs." She plays with my hair at the nape of my neck. During the off-season, I've let it grow out. I'm thinking of keeping it because she likes to tug on it when she's about to climax and I sort of like the feeling. "Well, not the editors, but Valentine's. She's really good at her job and making sure local bookstores know when someone in their area is releasing a book."

"So, what happens at this book thing?"

"The signing?"

I nod.

"Well, you'll be the center of attention." She laughs. "You'll do a reading, answer some questions, and then you'll sit at a table and sign their copies."

I blow out an exaggerated gust of hot air. It's one thing

to be on TV but I'm surrounded by greatness and people are more focused on them than me. To have everyone fixated on me—I don't know how I feel about that.

"This sounds like a lot of pressure."

"You'll be fine," Kelsey tells me. "I'll be right there with you every step of the way."

"You won't leave my side?"

She shakes her head. "Nope. Valentine and Russ will be there as well. You'll have your entire publishing team, as well as your football team there to support you." Kelsey kisses me softly. "The kids are going to love you, Alex. You really did an amazing job on this book."

"It wouldn't have happened without you" Pulling her into my side, I say, "I love you. I can't thank you enough for this opportunity."

"Only the best for my guy. I love you too, Alex. You really rocked this book. Everyone is going to love it."

I'M NERVOUS.

Every time I look out, there are more and more kids waiting to meet me. Waiting for me to come out there and read to them. I can't recall the last time I read to anyone, other than Kelsey. I shouldn't be nervous though. I've done meet and greets a thousand times over, this should be easy.

Valentine comes toward me with a bright smile. She's someone who really enjoys her job, which I suppose for what she does, that's a good thing.

"Are you ready, Alex?"

"I think so."

She nods in encouragement. "They're very excited to meet you. Remember, they already know you as a football player, so you need to just go out there and be yourself."

"Easier said than done." Kelsey rubs her hand up and down my back to soothe me.

"I'll be right there with you," Valentine says. "And your team is out there."

"And I'll be out there too," Kelsey says.

"All right, let's do this."

Valentine goes first and then I follow with Kelsey right behind me. My team claps for me as soon as they see me. Not everyone is there, but most of them are, and some brought their kids. I shake hands, give hugs, and fight back a wave of tears. They're proud of me. Hell, I'm proud of what I accomplished.

Valentine leads me to the metal chair in front of everyone. I sit and smile at the kids. I don't know why I'm nervous, I've done these types of things a million times over, but this is different. They're here because of something I wrote. Sure, they know me from being a Pioneer. Now they'll know me as being an author—one that teaches them the ins and outs of the game I love, along with how to play it safely. I wave at the kids, smile, and sit down.

"Wow, so many of you came today," I start with. "I'm really happy to see you and thankful to your parents for bringing you."

Valentine hands me a copy of my book. I hold it up so everyone can see the front cover. It's a cartoonish looking kid who is meant to look like me. Word around the publishing house is that they're looking to turn him into a stuffed character, along with offering me a deal to write a series of books—if everything goes well.

I open the book and start reading. I find that I like it and seem to know when to change my voice. Maybe this is a side hustle or a career for down the road when I can no longer play or maybe I'll become a voice actor. I can do sexy like the men I hear Kelsey listening too.

After I say the last word, I close the book and set it on my lap. Almost immediately hands go up with questions. As much as I want to answer them all, I can't, and Valentine steps in.

"Alex is going to go sit at the table and sign books at the long table there. Line up, in a single file line, and have your questions ready."

"Miss?" a little boy calls out. "Will the other guys sign our books as well?"

I look over my shoulder at my teammates and each of them nod. I don't know if they'll ever understand how much their support means to me right now. Valentine sees this and motions for one of the store attendants. It's like they already know and have more tables and chairs coming out.

We make our way over to the table. She dishes out orders to some of the people around us about needing more pens. I'm told to sit in the third chair, with Russ next to me and Valentine in the first chair. I glance around for Kelsey and find her right behind me, holding pens.

"You've got this," she says and then blows a kiss in my direction.

One of the employees from the store puts a stack of books on the table in front of Valentine, and another sets multiple boxes next to her. I look over my shoulder at Kelsey who steps forward.

"There's a line of kids outside, but the store is at capacity."

"Oh, wow."

"You did good," Kelsey says. "What may have started

out as a ploy to see me has turned into something kids want. You should be proud."

"I am. I should thank the author of the football romance."

Kelsey laughs. "Why's that?"

"Because if it wasn't for her, I would've never met you, and meeting you has been the best thing to ever happen to me. I owe her."

"Well, you'll get your chance to thank her because she's here. Her next book, which I've already contracted, is about the center of her football team and how he falls for a woman who doesn't know anything about football."

I can't help but laugh. "Art imitating reality. I love it."

"Me too."

Before I sign my first book, I stand and pull Kelsey into my arms. If it wasn't for her, none of this would've happened. Actually, I have a whole lot of people to thank, but mostly the piece of paper that declared me a winner. I've never loved being a loser so much until now.

*** 

—> BONUS CONTENT <—
Wanna chat Beaumont Men, Books, and all other things?
Join The Beaumont Daily on Facebook!
Don't forget to follow me on Amazon, so you know when my next book comes out!
Thanks for reading.

# Family

## THE BEAUMONT SERIES

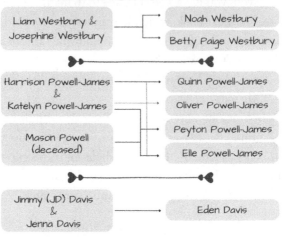

Liam Westbury &
Josephine Westbury

→ Noah Westbury

→ Betty Paige Westbury

Harrison Powell-James
&
Katelyn Powell-James

Mason Powell
(deceased)

→ Quinn Powell-James

→ Oliver Powell-James

→ Peyton Powell-James

→ Elle Powell-James

Jimmy (JD) Davis
&
Jenna Davis

→ Eden Davis

## THE BEAUMONT SERIES
### (Next Generation)

Noah Westbury &
Peyton Powell-James

Ben Miller &
Elle Powell-James

Quinn Powell-James &
Nola Boone

Ajay Ballard &
Jameson Foster

→ Evelyn Ballard

→ James Ballard

# Tree

## THE PORTLAND PIONEERS

Elena Cunningham

Julius Cunningham &
Autumn LaRossa

→ Reggie Cunningham

→ Roxy Cunningham

→ Julius Jr (JJ)
Cunningham

Alex Moore &
Kelsey Stone

## THE BEAUMONT SERIES
### (Novellas & Spin-offs)

Nick Ashford &
Aubrey Ashford

→ Mack Ashford

→ Amelie Ashford

Yvie James &
Xander Knight

Eden Davies &
Rush Fennimore

## ALSO BY HEIDI MCLAUGHLIN

THE BEAUMONT SERIES

Forever My Girl

My Everything

My Unexpected Forever

Finding My Forever

Finding My Way

12 Days of Forever

My Kind of Forever

Forever Our Boys

Forever Mason

The Beaumont Boxed Set - #1

THE BEAUMONT SERIES: NEXT GENERATION

Holding Onto Forever

My Unexpected Love

Chasing My Forever

Peyton & Noah

Fighting For Our Forever

Give Me Forever

A Beaumont Family Christmas

THE PORTLAND PIONEERS:

A BEAUMONT SERIES NEXT GENERATION

SPIN-OFF

Fourth Down

Fair Catch

False Start

CAPE HARBOR SERIES

After All

Until Then

THE ARCHER BROTHERS

Here with Me

Choose Me

Save Me

Here with Us

Choose Us

The Archer Boxset

LOST IN YOU SERIES

Lost in You

Lost in Us

THE BOYS OF SUMMER

Third Base

Home Run

Grand Slam

Hawk

THE REALITY DUET

Blind Reality

Twisted Reality

SOCIETY X

Dark Room

Viewing Room

Play Room

THE CLUTCH SERIES

Roman

STANDALONE NOVELS

Stripped Bare

Blow

Sexcation

HOLIDAY NOVELS

Santa's Secret

It's a Wonderful Holiday

THE DATING SERIES

A Date for Midnight

A Date with an Admirer

A Date for Good Luck

A Date for the Hunt

A Date for the Derby

A Date to Play Fore

A Date with a Foodie

A Date for the Fair

A Date for the Regatta

A Date for the Masquerade

A Date with a Turkey

A Date with an Elf

# ABOUT HEIDI MCLAUGHLIN

Heidi McLaughlin is a New York Times, Wall Street Journal, and USA Today Bestselling author of The Beaumont Series, The Boys of Summer, and The Archers.

In 2012, Heidi turned her passion for reading into a full-fledged literary career, writing over twenty novels, including the acclaimed Forever My Girl.

Heidi's first novel, Forever My Girl, has been adapted into a motion picture with LD Entertainment and Roadside Attractions, starring Alex Roe and Jessica Rothe, and opened in theaters on January 19, 2018.

*Don't miss more books by Heidi McLaughlin! Sign up for her newsletter, join the fun in her fan group, or get text updates. Text GETHEIDISBOOKS to (833) 926-1009!*

*Connect with Heidi!*
www.heidimclaughlin.com

Made in United States
North Haven, CT
03 September 2023

41089577R00154